76th Annual Writer's Digest Writing Competition

COLLECTION

The Grand-Prize and First-Place Manuscripts in Each Category of the 76th Annual *Writer's Digest* Writing Competition

90068 • *Writer's Digest* • 4700 East Galbraith Road • Cincinnati, OH 45236

These are works of fiction and nonfiction. As applicable, the events and characters described herein are imaginary and are not intended to refer to specific places or living persons. The opinions expressed in this manuscript are solely the opinions of the authors and do not represent the opinions or thoughts of the publisher or *Writer's Digest*.

The 76th Annual *Writer's Digest* Writing Competition Collection
All Rights Reserved
Copyright © 2007 *Writer's Digest* magazine

The selections printed herein reflect the authors' original manuscripts as submitted to the 76th Annual *Writer's Digest* Writing Competition.

This book may not be reproduced, transmitted, or stored in whole or in part by any means, including graphic, electronic, or mechanical without the express written consent of the publisher except in the case of brief quotations embodied in critical articles and reviews.

Outskirts Press
http://www.outskirtspress.com

ISBN: 978-1-4327-1016-3

Outskirts Press and the "OP" logo are trademarks belonging to Outskirts Press, Inc.

PRINTED IN CANADA

INTRODUCTION

The editors of *Writer's Digest* are pleased to share with you the winning entries in each category of the 76th Annual *Writer's Digest* Writing Competition, along with the Grand Prize-winning story, "The Salamander Prayer," by Eros-Alegra Clarke.

A special thanks goes to our esteemed panel of final-round judges:
- **Dorianne Laux** (Non-Rhyming Poetry) is the author of four books of poetry, most recently *Facts about the Moon* (W.W. Norton, 2005), winner of the Oregon Book Award. She is also co-author of *The Poet's Companion: A Guide to the Pleasures of Writing Poetry* (W.W. Norton, 1997). She is a professor at the University of Oregon and also teaches at Pacific University's Low Residency Program in Forest Grove, Oregon.
- **Carol Moldaw** (Rhyming Poetry) is the author of three books of poetry: *The Lightning Field*, winner of the 2002 FIELD Poetry Prize, *Chalkmarks on Stone*, and *Taken from the River*, as well as a chapbook, *Through the Window*. A recipient of a Pushcart Prize and a NEA Creative Writing Fellowship, Moldaw's work has been widely published in journals, including *Chicago Review, Colorado Review, Conjunctions, Denver Quarterly, The New Republic, The New Yorker, Paris Review, Parnassus, The Threepenny Review* and *Triquarterly*. Her lyric novel, *The Widening*, will be published in March 2008.
- **Warren Littlefield** (TV/Movie Script) spent 10 years as president of NBC Entertainment, where he was responsible for the development of such shows as "Seinfeld," "Friends," "Will & Grace" and "ER." He currently heads the Littlefield Company, where he's produced "Do Over" (WB), "Keen Eddie" (FOX), "Like Family" (WB) and "Love, Inc." (UPN).
- **Jerry B. Jenkins** (Inspirational) is a novelist, biographer, and marriage and family author who has been featured on the cover of *Newsweek*. He has written more than 160 books, and his writing has appeared in *Time, Reader's Digest*, and dozens of other periodicals. He owns Jenkins Entertainment (a filmmaking company) and the Christian Writers Guild.
- **J.A. Konrath** (Mainstream/Literary Short Story) is the author of the Lt. Jacqueline "Jack" Daniels thriller series. His work has appeared in more than 40 anthologies and magazines.
- **Christina Hamlett** (Stageplay), a former actress and director, is an award-winning author and professional script consultant whose credits

to date include 25 books, 125 plays and musicals, five optioned feature films and columns that appear in trade publications and online websites throughout the world. She and her husband reside in Pasadena, California.

- **Nancy Bilyeau** (Feature Article) is a deputy editor of *InStyle* magazine. She's also been an editor at *Ladies' Home Journal, Good Housekeeping, Rolling Stone, Men's Journal, Healthy Living, Mademoiselle* and *American Film*. She wrote a chapter for Therese J. Borchard's *The Imperfect Mom: Candid Confessions of Mothers Living in the Real World* (Broadway).

- **David Vann** (www.davidvann.com) (Memoir/Personal Essay) is author of the bestseller *A Mile Down: The True Story of a Disastrous Career at Sea*. He has features forthcoming in *Esquire, Men's Journal, Outside*, and *Outside's GO*, and his work has also appeared in *The Atlantic Monthly, Writer's Digest*, and other magazines and won various awards. He's been a Wallace Stegner Fellow, taught at Stanford and Cornell, and is now a professor at FSU.

- **Jennifer Crusie** (jennycrusie.com) (Genre Short Story) is the *New York Times, USA Today* and *Publishers Weekly* bestselling author of 17 novels, one book of literary criticism, miscellaneous articles, essays, novellas, and short stories, and the editor of three essay anthologies. She lives on the Ohio River.

- **Alice Pope** (cwim.blogspot.com) (Children's) has been editor of *Children's Writer's & Illustrator's Market* for 15 years. She also serves as Managing Editor of Writer's Digest Books Market Books department; edits other Writer's Digest Books titles; is a former Regional Advisor for the Society of Children's Books Writers and Illustrators; and is a regular speaker at writing conferences during which she has critiqued hundreds of manuscripts. Alice is on the editorial staff of *Fresh Boiled Peanuts: A Literary Journal* and is co-author of *The Writer's Book of Matches*.

We'd also like to acknowledge our first-round judges, who evaluated more than 19,000 entries: **Miriam Sagan** (Non-Rhyming Poetry), **James Cummins** (Rhyming Poetry), **Chad Gervich** (TV/Movie), **Ann Byle** (Inspirational), **Debby Mayne** (Mainstream/Literary Short Story), **Aury Wallington** (Stageplay), **Jordan E. Rosenfeld** (Feature Article), **Hollis Gillespie** (Memoir/Personal Essay), **Julie Wheeler** (Genre Short Story), and **Liza N. Burby** (Children's).

Finally, our most heartfelt congratulations to the winners and the entrants in this year's competition. The quality of your entries makes the judging more difficult each year. We look forward to seeing your work in the 77th Annual *Writer's Digest Writing Competition Collection*.

TABLE OF CONTENTS

Grand-Prize Winner
THE SALAMANDER PRAYER — 4
EROS-ALEGRA CLARKE

Children's/Young Adult Fiction Winner
NOT IN THE SCRIPT — 8
AMY J. FINNEGAN

Feature Article Winner
TERRY NORBLOM IS LOOKING FOR SOMETHING — 12
KATIE MCCOLLOW

Genre Short Story Winner
OPTICAL ILLUSION — 16
SUZANNE BURNS

Inspirational Writing Winner
ON KISSING AGAIN WITH TEARS — 23
BRADLEY J. GUSTAFSON

Mainstream/Literary Short Story Winner
NOTHING AT ALL IS MORE THAN ENOUGH — 27
JEFF MCCORMICK

Memoir/Personal Essay Winner
DISABILITY AND THE DESIRE FOR LOVE — 36
TODD GAUCHAT WITH DEBORAH BURKE

Non-Rhyming Poetry Winner
THE QUILTS FROM GEE'S BEND, ALABAMA — 40
ALISON LUTERMAN

Rhyming Poetry Winner
THE ASIAN MARKET — 41
JAMES ANDERSON

Stage Play Winner
HUNGARIAN RHAPSODY: AN ELECTROGLIDE IN BLUE — 42
DON ORWALD

Television/Movie Script Winner
CUT — 59
MAUREEN OLUND

GRAND-PRIZE WINNER

THE SALAMANDER PRAYER

Eros-Alegra Clarke
Cambria, CA

On the last day of camp I took home of a jar of salamanders. I stole them really. Looking back, I don't know how I managed it.

Salamanders were abundant in the Camp Ketapalunka swimming lake. There was a group of boys who killed them for fun. Others died by mistake. There were so many of us kids in that lake it was hard for the salamanders to not get kicked or smashed. Their lime green bodies and hungry webbed hands would come floating to the surface—always on a place somewhere along the delicate body there would be a tear, a place where inside had broken through.

They did not bleed how we bleed. They bled thickly. It did not kindly spread itself out and disappear. It coiled like spaghetti and only journeyed so far away from its home.

I would look away from these discarded bodies and feel the waste of it. I wanted their secrets and they had been carelessly crushed.

I had a need to possess and protect these salamanders. I believed that they would share their secrets. I wanted more than the world I knew. A place where air was unnecessary and gravity did not hold me.

I convinced my parents to let me dig a hole in the backyard. A hole lined with black plastic garbage bags and filled with water taken from the still places in the reservoir. It would have the sort of things that an underworld would need: food and snails and a jungle of water-breathing plants that sway like hair. Among these things I would learn to swim, without breathing, without blinking.

I would glide.

My movement would be silent music.

There would be no death, no broken bodies, no spilling of secret things.

I was shaping a prayer.

My plan of rescuing the salamanders was carried out on the last day of camp. As kids chased each other into the water, I weaved among them carrying an empty mayonnaise jar wrapped in a towel.

I walked at odd angles and used the loud cries and blurred bodies of my peers for camouflage. I waded into the deep water of the lake where all movement quieted. I held the jar beneath the surface and the salamanders came to me.

There was a power in how effortless it had been.

I waited for the day to end, the hours stretched until they were so thin I thought the afternoon might tear and then it was time to go home.

I had done it. I had stolen my salamanders.

When I saw my mother I resolved to keep my mouth shut. I couldn't risk ruining the power of the secret by letting an adult in on it. I began to talk the moment I collapsed into the passenger seat of our blue Volkswagen bug. My mouth won't close. I try to force it shut but the words wiggle between my teeth and I am powerless.

"I've got four and they're in here," I point to my backpack.

My mother doesn't say anything. She is concentrating on pulling out onto the main road. My mother does not like to drive. My tongue twists against my mouth. I am sure I have ruined the power of my secret. The words float around us in the car. I don't need to say anything more, I tell myself. Wait until she asks. I look ahead as if I am concentrating on something.

My mouth opens and it all begins again.

"One of the counselors said there are so many of them, that really there are too many of them and that it is good some of them are going to a home."

I watch the telephone poles go by. My words echo, bouncing against my skull, embarrassing me. My mother doesn't say anything but I can feel her smile growing.

A boy in a red hooded sweatshirt and blue pants rides by on a bicycle. He is bent over the handlebars, pedaling hard. For a moment I see his face. His mouth is pulled tightly together and his forehead is creased. I do not notice right away that the day is too hot for his clothes. I only notice that something in his face makes me feel lonely.

"Well…" I can hear the smile in my mother's voice. I ignore it. "Those salamanders couldn't have found their way into the hands of a better little girl. I am sure they will love their new home."

"Yeah," I say, "because they'll be safe. They won't have to die."

My mother takes her eyes off the road and I scrunch into the seat, fixing my eyes on the road so that we won't crash. I want her to be the one watching, it's hard work controlling the car from where I am.

"Honey, they'll die some day, it's natural."

"No, they won't." I glance at the side mirror. I can see the boy pedaling in the heat and dust. He is small now and growing smaller. Soon he will disappear. I pull at the waistband of my shorts, they snap back against my skin and make my flesh feel spongy, like I am absorbing the heat and swelling up. I don't like it.

"What was that honey?"

I don't say anything. She doesn't get it. They won't die—they can't die. That's the whole point. I want to scream this but I sit there silent, feeling my skin shrink.

5

The salamanders make a cool thunking noise against the jar. The sound makes my heart feel too big for my body. I love the salamanders. It hurts.

"You do realize that you can't keep them forever. Nothing is forever. Everything lives for a certain amount of time, but you can enjoy them for that time and give them the best life you can."

I can tell she is trying to give me something, but she doesn't understand that if I accept it, I am losing something, so I close my ears and wait for her to stop.

I want to tell her that dying isn't always about having things leak out of us. It is important to not break the surface that keeps inside from the outside, but that is just the beginning. Not dying is about being able to remember the right thing at the right time, to remember some things all the time so that if something threatens to break our surface, it won't matter, it won't matter if our insides leak out.

Like the girl behind the pizza place.

I wasn't supposed to know about her but I found out. She was only a year or two older than me.

She had been stabbed 100 times.

I couldn't stop thinking about her, I wanted to know if she was able to remember, if while her outside was being broken did her insides remain.

Was she able to hold onto her story?

I wanted to know if I would be able to remember. If I were lying on cold earth with a knife and a man above me, would I be able to look at the stars and not lose myself in the horror of his eyes?

She was young, but maybe too old to remember. Too old to hold on to those stars so that fear would not steal everything—so that when they found her buried beneath piles of dirty aprons, they found more than a murdered child, they found a body with a soul that had leaked out, rather than risen.

One night in bed I counted to a hundred because I didn't believe there was room on one body to be stabbed that many times.

Counting to a hundred, a hundred slashes, I ran out of space on my body.

I began sleeping on my stomach because I thought that it would be too hard for someone to stab through the bones of my back. It would be too much effort. But I didn't want to depend on those things, I wanted to know that if I became that girl, I would be able to look at the stars and see only the stars. If there were men that would bury a girl beneath dirty aprons behind a pizza parlor, I wanted an escape route from this world.

I waited until sunset to release my salamander prayers.

When the light was gold and slanted across everything so that it caught the edges of leaves, blades of grass, and made everything glow, that was when I took the salamanders out into the back yard.

I sat by the pond, the sun creeping over my skin, the way sleep crept over me. It tucked me in beneath its warm blanket but instead of sleep, this time of day made me want to play, to go exploring.

The air smelled of summer barbeques. I could hear other children laughing in their yards. There were adult voices drifting through the trees, raining down around me. I breathed it in and opened the mayonnaise jar, releasing the salamanders. They looked up at me with soft black eyes. Their mouths looked like smiles. I wanted to trace the gentle lines of their bodies. It made my stomach tighten, the way they were so fragile. But they would be safe now. I would feed them. I would watch over them. I would love them.

The circular drone of crickets had begun to spiral out from the corners of the yard. Soon I would be able to hear the frogs from the reservoir, the two choirs weaving together like a lullaby.

I wondered if the girl behind the pizza parlor had heard the crickets. I wondered if she had cried out for her parents. If she had been able to hear the sound of children's laughter in yards that must have felt a million miles away. Had it been the sound of traffic that drowned her calls for help? Did the man's shadow smother her so that all she could hear was his threat?

I didn't want the stars to be cold and distant for her that night. I wanted the light to have crept across her; I wanted the song of crickets to have surrounded her. I wanted to believe that she wasn't alone when what was inside broke through to the outside.

I wanted to believe that her outside bled into the world and joined it:
Joined the smell of lilacs blossoming on summer trees.
Joined crocuses as they pushed their way through dark earth.
Joined the smell of melting cheese and laughter.
That her insides had escaped from the monster and found their way to that place where children adventure along new paths that sometimes lead through dark woods—a place where the children become something more than children along the way.

They do not forget.
They remember.
And they return with stories; stories to be read to other children. Children snuggled beneath blankets with bellies full of warm milk.

I sank the mayonnaise jar into the pond. The pond I had dug with my mother's help. My father had lined it with the plastic, promising me it would be safe, that the water would not escape back into the earth, and it didn't.

The water was dark as the salamanders slipped silently, one by one away from me. I hugged my knees to my chest and waited. The sky was turning a color that I had no name for, but it was warm and beautiful and it made my eyelids feel heavy. I waited until I saw them appear, one by one. The salamanders surfaced, to look at me with their round black eyes. Eyes liquid like the night, eyes that reflected dreams. They looked at me with their mouths like smiles and then one by one they sunk back into the shadows.

CHILDREN'S/YOUNG ADULT FICTION WINNER

NOT IN THE SCRIPT

Amy J. Finnegan
Highland, UT

"What a joke. *Celebrity Weekly* has just 'confirmed' that I'm dating Troy again," I said, skimming the pages of a tabloid—one of many that were scattered around my best friend's bedroom. "He'll be happy to hear that. I haven't returned a single call from him in months."

"I'd feel bad for you, Emma, but some of us aren't fortunate enough to have guys to ignore," Rachel said. She was lying on her bed, staring at pictures of her favorite pinup boy. She'd christened him The Bod—an appropriate name for an underwear model. "But it's just as well, since The Bod is the only guy I'm dying to be with, and he doesn't even know I exist."

"I doubt he's worth dying for," I said. "When heaven gives a guy a body like that, it shorts him on brain cells." I had to agree with her on one thing though; he made cowboy chaps look hot. "And his arrogance couldn't help much. Just look at that smirk. I bet his puffy lips are airbrushed."

"Why would you say that, Emma? His lips are like soft pillows, not puffy." She seemed offended, as if she actually knew the guy, or even his name. "And for a girl who was just ranked as one of the Most Beautiful Young Celebrities, you're awfully critical of beautiful people."

I had been at Rachel's all afternoon, waiting for my agent to send an e-mail about the casting choices for the new series I'd be starting soon. I was more nervous than I had been in a long time over a role. I hadn't worked with many actors my age, but with a teen drama series that was sure to change.

"All I'm saying is that men who look like The Bod are the most overrated gimmicks on the planet," I said, clicking through pages of the Unofficial Emma Taylor Fansite. "Unofficial" was right. Like I'd ever give my permission for strangers to judge me on everything from a new haircut, to the way my butt looked in different styles of jeans. Not to mention their ever-so-wrong take on my personal life.

"You only think that because hot guys make you psychotic," said Rachel. She turned her attention to the web page that I'd been reading earlier. "So, what do your cyber-stalkers have to say about you today?"

"Let's see," I said, finding the newest post on the message board. It was written by someone with the username EmmaWantsMe. Pahleeesseee. I read the post for Rachel:

> I'm the kind of guy Emma's looking for. 1) I'm 6'1" and she says that she likes tall guys. 2) I have blonde hair. Her last three boyfriends

were blonde, so that's a given. 3) My IQ is above 140 (genius range, if you're unaware). 4) I'm a freshman at Stanford—close enough to jet down for her LA premieres, whenever duty calls. 5) I'm rich. My parents own eight Napa Valley vineyards. With all that, why wouldn't Emma fall in love with me?

"How audacious," I said, warming up my hands. "I hope he's expecting an answer, because he's gonna get one." Under Rachel's username, TheBodIsMine, I replied:

EmmaWantsMe, I think you may be a few donuts short of a dozen. Emma has dumped all three of her blonde boyfriends—who were also rich and over six feet tall. But it's great that you'll inherit some cash from your wealthy parents. I bet they've worked hard to give you the lifestyle you deserve. And being seventeen, Emma can't drink wine yet, or I'm sure she'd be impressed with the vineyard bit. So that only leaves your intelligence to stand on, and I have to wonder just how bright a guy is to use his IQ score as chick bait. Sorry to burst your bubble, dude, but Emma would be better off dating a troll.

When I submitted the post, Rachel slapped my arm. "I thought you'd erase that," she said with a huff. "I had a decent reputation on this site before you came along."

It was the type of message I usually wrote to vent, then went heavy on the backspace key, but this guy had caught me on the wrong day. "I just told him not to waste his time." Rachel was still giving me her how-could-you look. "Okay, if he responds, I'll apologize. I'll even send him an autographed photo."

"No, you won't."

I shrugged. "Well, he needs something to look at besides his own reflection. Right?"

My e-mail inbox made a clicking sound and I opened it, certain I was about to discover who my new best friends would be—at least while cameras were rolling. I read the message from my agent out loud. " 'Executive Producer Steve McGregor will begin filming the pilot of *Coyote Hills*...in Tucson, Arizona. Please report to Desert Productions Studios for the first rehearsal'... blah blah blah...sorry, Rachel, gotta find the good stuff...oh, here it is... 'The role of Ellie will be played by Emma Taylor, the role of Justin is still in negotiations'— right, I bet they're having casting issues—moving on...'The role of Kassidy will be played by Kimmi Carlson, and the role of Bryce will be played by'—" I choked on my tongue. "What the...no!" I was so horrified that I pushed the power button on the monitor.

"What's wrong?" asked Rachel. "Is it someone you've worked with before?"

My heart was on hyper-drive. "Worse, much worse."

She bumped me to the edge of the chair as she sat, then turned the monitor back on. "What are you freaking out about...no way!" She bounced up and down, her golden hair bouncing with her. "I can't believe it!"

9

I stood, surprised my legs could hold me. "Please stop. This is a nightmare."

"No, it's not! It's fate!" Rachel said, her green eyes bulging. "You've had a thing for Brett Cooper since you were like ten!"

"Exactly!" I collapsed into her pile of bed pillows and threw my hands over my face. "Which means I can't work with him."

"Of course you can. And even better, you can date him."

Had Rachel's brain been on vacation for the last two years of my life? "I'd rather suffocate myself with this pillow," I told her.

Even putting aside my own mistakes of falling for cast members, I knew all too well that on-set romances were, more often than not, total disasters. Until last spring I was in a primetime drama that was cancelled due to conflict on the set. I played the President's daughter, but this particular president—who, one year earlier had truly married the actress who played the First Lady—was discovered to be having an affair with our executive producer's wife. It wasn't pretty. A studio can't fire both the President and First Lady, and still call the show *The First Family*. I would've suggested an impeachment storyline, but when the President goes, so does his daughter. Either way, I was out of a job.

That's when Steve McGregor, the do-it-all executive producer/writer/director of *Coyote Hills*, called my agent. It was the very day the cancellation of my show was announced and I hadn't received a greater compliment in the five years of my career. McGregor was responsible for more hit dramas than any producer in television.

A dozen actors had already warned me that McGregor was a nutcase, but I'd worked with enough chaotic geniuses to know that there was no use questioning their methods. Unique minds blow audiences away. So nutcases I could handle—no problem. But working with a guy I'd been drooling over since I was old enough to drool? No way!

"Why would Brett want to come back to television?" I asked Rachel. "He's been doing so well on the big screen."

"Don't you keep up with anything?" she said. "It's amazing how much more I know about your world than you do."

"Just give me the scoop, please."

"Well, according to insiders, Brett's been a pain to work with lately. He misses call times and keeps the cast and crew waiting for hours." She sounded like a newscaster, and even held up a magazine as if it was hard evidence. "Critics say that he's lost his passion for acting—that he'll be nothing but a washed-up child star if he doesn't do something to redeem himself."

"Redeem himself?" I asked with narrowed eyes. "Everyone knows what a fantastic actor Brett is. He's probably just burned out from working so hard."

"Maybe," Rachel said. "But don't you think there might be a sliver of truth to the other rumors, too? There's a new one every week."

Of course there could be some truth behind the stories. But when it came to media rumors, I'd trained myself to believe the opposite. "Rachel, tabloids are pure trash." My skin crawled as I thought of the lies attached to me. "I've proven that a hundred times over."

"Come on, Em," she said. "Brett's obviously distracted by other things right now, including his horde of women. And I just read an article that said he hasn't had a single job offer in six months."

"Then I guess McGregor is the only producer who can see past rumors and focus on talent," I told her, massaging my throbbing head. Brett had just turned twenty; he had every right to explore things outside the Hollywood studio he'd been locked in since he was four. But that didn't mean I wanted to date him. I'd even gone out of my way to avoid meeting him.

Rachel drummed her fingers. "You're right, you can't work with this guy. You'll totally flip if he turns out to be a jerk."

"No, I won't," I said, but knew I wouldn't be hyperventilating if that weren't a possibility. "I just like the Brett Cooper that exists in my imagination, even if it's not how he really is. He's always been someone safe to crush on, you know?" Something had just hit me. "And why are you saying how awful Brett is if you think fate has brought us together?"

Her lips curled up. "Because he's gonna fall head over heels for you, and then he'll change his whole life." Whoever coined the term "drama queen" must've met Rachel.

"You're crazy if you think I want to be Brett Cooper's next 'Throw-away Party Favor.'" I felt like I should put soap in my mouth for quoting a tabloid writer, but it shot me back to reality. "And I'll never date another guy I work with. It's not worth risking my career."

"But wouldn't you give up anything for love? Like real love."

"Hmm, let's see…nope."

"Yes, you would," Rachel said. "So if Brett sweeps you off your feet, give him a chance. You can't be a bitter hag forever."

"I'm not a bitter hag, I just don't want to deal with Brett right now," I said, trying to brush off how rude that was. She had no idea how bad things were with Troy in the end, and I thought I was handling things pretty well. "This new job is a fresh start for me, and I don't want to mess it up. Do you really think you could focus at work if The Bod was standing next to you?"

Rachel turned back to her wall, glowing. "I know exactly what I'd be focusing on."

I couldn't help but laugh at her silly expression. "The Bod's all yours, sweetie," I said, just as I'd told her a dozen times before. "I guess I'll just have to get over my own dream guy—like, really fast." But even after reading page after page of tabloid gossip, I still couldn't imagine Brett with a single flaw.

[EXCERPT FROM A YOUNG ADULT NOVEL]

FEATURE ARTICLE WINNER

TERRY NORBLOM IS LOOKING FOR SOMETHING

Katie McCollow
Minneapolis, MN

They used to call him "Scary Terry," back in the day when he was in fighting trim; 150 pounds of wild-eyed, pony-tailed sinew. The still pictures on the wall of his kickboxing gym show him applying a side kick to his hapless opponent's chin, every muscle in his ropy body standing on high alert.

Watching the video footage of his fights, the speed and precision of his kicks are awesome indeed. His legs seemingly fly out of nowhere, whirling and spinning in a blink-and-you-missed-it way, leaving his challengers stunned and defeated. He gets impossibly elevated, like a character from *Crouching Tiger, Hidden Dragon* only there aren't any wires in evidence and I don't fall asleep before the fights are over. Scary Terry.

Terry Norblom can still seem pretty scary. He's packing a few more pounds and a lot less hair than he had when he was the U.S. Kickboxing champion in 1986; perhaps no longer as lithe and limber but still quite fit and strong as an ox. Punch a pad he's holding, and you'll feel the reverb up in your shoulder and down your back, as if you've just hit a brick wall.

He's been teaching ten kickboxing classes and eighteen karate classes a week for the past 30 years, every session a one-man show in which he bellows and inspires; along with technical instruction, a barrage of free-wheeling, free-thinking philosophies fly off the top of his head with all the agility and momentum that used to define his kicks. His mental gymnastics are as impressive as his physical ones used to be.

When he's firing on all cylinders, think Mr. Clean on Red Bull and Nietzsche. But when the hour is over, he goes into his figurative tent and the carnival shuts down. He is a rock. He is an island. Approaching him with a question or a request can turn the most self-assured diva's colon to soup. Told he can be, ahem, intimidating, however, and he turns it back on you.

"I'm just being myself. You choose to be intimidated by me," he says with a vulpine grin.

Fair enough...pardon me for a moment, will you? I just chose to wet my pants.

Give him a spotlight and he's golden; fluent, easy speech comes naturally when he's in front of a crowd, not so much one on one. Then a muscle in his jaw twitches a little, his eyes dart uncomfortably around as if looking for the nearest exit. But ask him about his golf game and his shoulders visibly relax.

Inquire after his kids and he smiles, a real, genuine smile. His voice softens and he actually becomes chatty and tentatively cracks some jokes, and it becomes clear that despite his tough-guy exterior and outsized public persona, "intimidating" is indeed a misnomer; Terry Norblom is simply shy.

***

He's been searching for things, for discipline, meaning, connection, for a long time.

It's understandable, when you hear his story. He says his search started quite young, pre-school age, when his mother went to work full time and he was left "to figure things out for myself."

One of the things he figured out was that if he didn't want to go to school, all he had to do was fake sick and his busy mom would let him stay home.

Mild learning disabilities went ignored, and like unchecked weeds in a flower bed, the resulting lack of self-confidence took over and choked out the whole garden. He skipped school a lot, spent too much time alone.

He stayed home so much that by the end of ninth grade at his Bloomington, Minnesota, junior high, the school suggested he stay there for good.

He also figured out, in around seventh grade, that smoking pot was pretty fun. He spent most of his teen years in a stoned haze, hoping to find what he was looking for at the bottom of a hash pipe. Heroin and LSD were brought into the rotation.

On one particular night, while tripping on LSD, he smashed a half bottle of wine all over his parents' basement ceiling and ran obliviously through the glass. He sold drugs as well, had a nice little business going for a teenaged kid; "90 bucks a week and all the hash I could smoke."

Oftentimes where there are teens doing drugs, there are teens having sex, which led Terry to a search of another sort, for the daughter he fathered at 14 and gave up for adoption. The child had Downs Syndrome, and when he finally tracked her down, years later, her adoptive family felt it best she not be contacted, his hunt left incomplete.

A run-in with a bigger guy on a remote Montana highway combined with the popularity of Kung Fu movies on late-night television prompted him to take his first Karate class, one month shy of his seventeenth birthday. Martial arts require discipline and structure, two things his life lacked up to that point. He took to it like a thirsty desert nomad to an oasis, and he was good at it.

He was still getting into trouble, though; he was busted breaking and entering to steal back some drugs that were stolen from him. As part of the first-time offenders program, he had to get a job, and he got one, sweeping up the police station.

He couldn't get high before karate class, however, and one night found himself at a party where seemingly everyone was talking about how "f***** up" they were.

"I looked around at all of them and thought to myself, 'I don't want to get f***** up, and I don't want to be here.'"

He quit doing drugs. He got his G.E.D. He set his sights on becoming a champion fighter and karate teacher.

"Karate saved my life," he says.

He got his black belt in 1977 and began teaching at The National Karate Schools, where he'd trained, soon afterward. During his ten years there, his students won more awards and he graduated more black belts than any other teacher.

***

Around the time he was training for the national kickboxing championship, he began developing a program for children.

He loved kids, and hit on the idea to go around to day care centers and teach karate. The first day, upon being confronted with a room full of rambunctious young'uns, he had to think on his feet and barked "Rule Number One! Listen!" and "Terry Norblom's Karate for Kids," his values-based martial arts program, was born, later shortened to the catchier "Kidratee."

Each class was broken into three basic components: A life lesson, such as kindness, accountability, or following through followed by physical exercise and a game that reinforced the life lesson.

The program was an instant success. The next year he added a summer camp where he would have the kids' undivided attention for a week.

"It's still my most effective week of the year," he says.

One very popular lesson he came up with at the camp was called "Parent Appreciation."

He assigned the littlest children to be in charge of the bigger kids and the counselors; they had to tie their shoes, feed them, do everything for them.

"See, taking care of someone is a hard job," he explained. "Your parents have a hard job."

The kids then had to come up with a way they could make their parents' job easier.

Another lesson he created back then and still uses is: "If I see a mess, I clean it up."

The kids apply this lesson to messes in the literal sense, to fights with their friends, to sloppy karate form. They are sometimes told, as an assignment, to write down a mess of any kind that they have cleaned up and report back about it at the next class.

Once the technical, physical aspects of each belt level are met, these are the types of tasks the kids must complete in order to get their belts.

"I think about what the colors of the belts mean to me, and I try to incorporate that into the lesson." The belt levels also dictate the sophistication of the life lessons. A child training for a white belt, the first level, must learn an accountability exercise, something as simple as making their own bed to finding their shoes in the morning.

One of the things a student working toward a black belt must think about is technique sparring, and how it is used in karate and otherwise. For example, in fighting, a technique can be thrown a certain way in order to bring the opponent closer or to keep them away. The students are encouraged to think of "sparring" techniques in real life they may unconsciously use to achieve the same figurative goals, in order to better their relationships with others.

"I figured I was a good teacher just from my years of training, but (my psychic) did a past-life regression on me and said she believed I was a good teacher because I'd been one a thousand years before, when I'd lived on a mountaintop."

Terry is prone to these types of statements. He hunts for answers everywhere, forever digging through his metaphysical pockets trying to find the keys.

So far, he's found that the keys to the success of his program are the keys to the children's success, period.

In 1993 Terry and a partner opened a gym, Jabz Kickboxing and Kidratee, and ever since that's where he can be found seven days a week, teaching kickboxing to adults and Kidratee to their children.

His young charges adore him; they know him as Kidratee Man, a perfect, comic book-ish name for a larger-than-life character. They love him because he's fun. He tosses them around with the ease of a Grizzly bear handling beanie babies and can think up a new game on the fly, but more so because he expects things from them.

He expects them to listen, to follow directions, to not clown around and to not disrupt his class. He's more than willing to toss out kids he feels are being unruly, and more than willing to take them back the next week and give them endless chances to improve. But make no mistake, it's his way or the highway, and the kids learn it quickly and respond accordingly. They learn that in martial arts and in life, bad habits can get you in trouble.

It's a dying art, fearlessly disciplining children who get out of line. His classroom is a far cry from the sports fields of the modern child, where every kid who shows up is entitled to an unencumbered path to the hoop or the goal and a jumbo tub of high-fructose corn syrup after practice is over. But when Kidratee Man is pleased, the kids shine. They know they've earned their belts.

When his students break their first board, he inscribes it with "Keep on pivoting," pivoting being the most important aspect of a quality back kick.

Pivot, v: to turn or swing supported by a pivot

Pivot n 1: a small object such as a bar or pin that supports a larger object and lets it turn or swing

Pivot n 2: the one person or thing that is essential to the success or effectiveness of something.

Read the third definition, and Terry stares for a beat. "Wow," he says quietly.

"Believe me, I know I'm teaching the things I needed to learn the most."

And not-so-scary Terry will keep searching in his quest for lessons to impart, so his Kidratee kids won't have to look so hard.

GENRE SHORT STORY WINNER

OPTICAL ILLUSION

Suzanne Burns
Bend, OR

The day before my eye appointment, I had finally become invisible. It's not the kind of thing I'd recommend as a hobby. Garage saleing suits most women better, the way they hover over the flotsam and jetsam of second-hand junk with that ability to transform different teacups or bottles or even doorknobs into a collection. It's the way they display their knickknacks in shadowboxes with the thick wood frames that make anything look important. When I was nearly invisible, I had a hard time buying one of those frames because no one ever rushes over to help a shadow of a former self, no matter what the commission.

People used to notice me wherever I went. The cashier at the grocery store, the one with the freckles, always gave me correct change. Freckles give you a free pass to never disappear. So do accents, eyebrows like a young Elizabeth Taylor, the ability to rebuild engines and bake bread. And being an eye doctor's receptionist can never hurt.

She wears a different pair of designer frames every time I walk by the downtown office. The green pair rimmed in fake diamonds seems to be her favorite. They were glinting around her eyes like tiny dressing room lights when I ran into her last year at the Starbucks next door. Since I was still half a person back then, she whispered to me that when you admit something is phony, like rhinestones, you free yourself from the guilt of pretending.

"But nothing about me is fake," I said. "I'm disappearing because I have nothing to hide behind."

On the day of my eye appointment I wore a dress so close to the color of my skin, I couldn't tell in the reflection from my bedroom window whether the sleeves were short or my arms were long. It had been months since I hid my mirror, training myself to do things like brush my teeth from memory. It's not like my molars and incisors were switching places anytime soon.

For being nearly invisible, I had one of the best views in town. In real estate ads they'd call my house quaint, but it's not the inside of anyplace that counts. It's how your house, through windows, on the back porch, looking out your front door, allows you to see the rest of the world. From the bluffs overlooking downtown I could watch people share sandwiches at a café, argue into cell phones, cut off the circulation in their hands from clutching a half-dozen shopping bags. Of course my favorite view was George, or at least the sun-faded roof of the building where he worked. Every year before I made my eye appointment, I asked if George would be there. It made the four-block walk to the office feel like floating.

When I checked in at the front desk, the yearly drill, the receptionist ignored me to drink tea out of a large Styrofoam cup. She keeps the tag of the teabag dangling towards the front door so I'll see that she doesn't even need to add caffeine to her perfect life.

The eye doctor went through the motions. The puff of air that makes me jump every time, the near lullaby of asking which lens is clearer, one or two. Like it's some sort of test, I always memorize the smallest row of letters on the wall chart. By the time the doctor catches on, she has already forgotten my name.

My disembodied, skin-colored dress made its way back through the waiting room, my body almost history until George reintroduced me to my flesh. My heart raced back. My arms shook. George eats organic food in his side office where he makes glasses for a living. I have never learned the technical name for this, but I know he went to school because a framed certificate watches over George as he grinds spectacles. I've learned something new about him each of the seven years he has adjusted my frames. George loves cats. George is a tri-athlete. George makes his own hummus, whatever that is. George tells me it's a very rare thirty-five-year-old woman whose prescription never changes. Here comes my superstar, he says every year, as if I have control over keeping my myopia in check. George treats these interactions like picnics, casual, deliberate yet fleeting. It's because George has no idea that he is the only person who has ever looked me in the eyes.

I mean really looked. He looks at me like he enjoys what he sees, like for those few minutes, we exist in a world separate from everyone else. He looks at me in a way that almost makes me want to reveal all the secrets no one should ever tell.

In books they describe limpid pools, but George's eyes are an unspectacular shade of brown. That's what he always says. Then he advises me to change my driver's license to say hazel. It's because of the olive tinge, he says, and for days after each visit I imagine Tuscan hills.

"There's another one with Stockholm Syndrome," the receptionist whispered to George at the end of my last appointment like I couldn't hear her when I browsed the new frames.

George asked fake diamond glasses, "Do you even know what that means?"

The receptionist sipped at her never-ending cup of tea. "It's when the patient falls in love with the doctor," she said.

"That's called transference," George told the girl, "and I'm nobody's doctor."

I continued poring over plastic frames in candy colors, trying to pick a new frame that would make me look like Audrey Hepburn, until I remembered that she never wore glasses.

"I'm on a break," George said in my direction while fake diamonds continued drinking her tea. "Why don't we go get coffee so I can apologize?"

At the café next door, George ordered two regular coffees and motioned for me to pick a table near the window. With each warm sip I felt a part of myself return. With each question George asked, his brown eyes fixed on mine with the sincerity of a dog, my substance appeared through a haze.

By the time he said, "I've always wanted to ask you out, but the doctor frowns on it," we were walking towards my house. George told me I was so pretty, he bet my skeleton was jealous of the way my muscles got to live right under my skin. George held me in the kind of spell you read about in true-crime novels. By the time I committed my own crime against him, though, I knew I'd never get caught.

Our walk up the bluffs turned into an early dinner and a late night. I didn't like kissing him so much or sleeping with him, because he kept his eyes closed the whole time. And whenever George closed his eyes, I disappeared.

We quickly became the kind of couple that enjoys making a scene. The public kissing. The feeding each other morsels of pastry over afternoon coffee while fake diamond glasses orders larger and larger cups of tea.

When my body finally came back, George took me shopping. We had dated for two months, long enough for the eye doctor and her receptionist to notice the sandwiches I packed for George's lunch on the sprouted wheat bread he liked so much, yet short enough, I thought, for my newly acquired figure to still stir him. I modeled dresses for George in boutiques that serve cappuccino while you shop, then jeans with intricate embroidery matched with those impossibly tight sweaters. My arms moved stiff as a robot from bracelets and watches and the kind of tooled leather cuffs young celebrities wear when they go clubbing. But no matter how much flash and glitter adorned me, I felt like George was somewhere else, gazing out the corner of his eye at any woman but me.

"It's all right," I told him over dinner that night. "They call it the two-month slump."

"You're crazy, Lavina. As soon as you give up the idea of vanishing, then you want me to disappear."

"That's not true." I kept squeezing a bottle of dressing over my salad.

"You'll ruin your arugula," George said.

"Well you're ruining this whole thing." I threw the bottle of dressing on the table. Oil and vinegar spattered my best flowered placemat. "For someone who saved my life, you sure didn't stay interested very long."

He did it again. George and his wandering eye. While his right eye focused on my drowned salad, the other seemed to turn towards the front door.

I yelled, "Why won't you pay attention to me?"

"But I haven't taken my eyes off you since we met." George shoved away his plate of spaghetti. Nothing could hold his attention as his gaze flitted from the noodles to me, back to the screen door.

I said, "Lately I feel like you're looking, but you aren't really seeing me. At least not all the way."

"Lavina, I think it's time I told you something."

This is it, I thought, he's leaving me for the receptionist. Even under her long wool skirts you could sense the outline of taut thighs. She was the kind of woman who could get away with wearing scarves. And the office florescence unwound blue veined ribbons beneath her skimmed cream skin. Most men have trained themselves to desire this translucence.

George bent over the table. He brought his hands towards his left eye like he was removing a contact lens. "I should've told you sooner, but I thought you'd figure it out."

I dumped his dinner in the trash. My oil-drenched salad wilted over his noodles. When I turned around, George held out his palm. He told me, "You can throw this away, too."

I moved close enough to see a piece of glass the size of a ping-pong ball sliced in half.

George said, "You can touch it if you want," then deposited the disc in my cupped hands. A white convex lens. Delicate pink tributaries branching out from its dark brown center. A glistening black dot waited at the middle of the small brown circle.

"This can't be," I folded my fingers around the glass to keep from staring, "an eye?"

"I had an accident so many years ago, I usually forget it's there." George kept his left eyelid shut. "More like I wish it wasn't. But it's not as obscene as you think. I have an implant, so it's not like there's a gaping hole or anything."

I wondered what George's eye socket looked like. Closing one of my eyes, I tried to see what he saw, realizing that the way he always pivoted his head towards me had nothing to do with one of my especially witty remarks. In a lesser variant of my disappearing act, George had lost his depth perception. On one of those interior-decorating shows I used to watch with all the free time that comes from fading away, its host kept referring to the visual field. If the vase on the end table is this tall, there had better be x many pillows fluffed in an asymmetric pattern over the corner setee. All the formulas I never understood until I started dating George. He seemed to take in my whole being with even a casual glance, his head front and center. I thought I was one of the lucky women who never has to lecture her man about his chronic habit of staring straight ahead when I am trying to make a point. George gave off the illusion of living in the moment.

I gripped the eye, my palms concealing the fixed iris, while I reflected on the gravity of this mute segment of glass. Recoiling from the prosthetic would anger George, and I had decided weeks before that if anyone was leaving each other, I was going first. And it wasn't like the eye felt gross. Just like the snakes they keep at the petting area of the kids' museum downtown feel more like rope than Vaseline. For the five-dollar admission, a corn snake with its bands of color will crawl all the way up your arm without leaving a sticky trail. The

19

goal is to teach children how nothing is ever what it seems.

I opened my palm to stare at the glass eye staring back at me. Maybe the receptionist was right about knowing when to admit something is fake. I told George, "And all this time I thought you brought me back."

"Back from where?"

"From the place most people never escape."

"Lavina, don't you know by now that I'd notice you without any eyes?"

I handed George his eye. He turned his back to insert it. Was that empty place in his head the color of bubblegum, or something even darker? As George faced me, I felt my body lose some of its definition. This could never be enough, loving a person who only sees me in one dimension. It almost felt worse than having never been seen at all.

Most girls grow up feeling like dolls. If I was a doll at all, it was the broken one at the bottom of the toy chest. George grew up at the top of the pile. King of the Hill climbing mountains of building blocks. His accident was the only reason why he slipped and fell down to me.

I asked, "Does fake diamonds know about your eye?"

"Who?"

"Christ, I mean the receptionist. Julie or something."

"Not unless Dr. Rogers told her."

"Well if the doctor knows, I'm sure Julie something knows."

We washed dishes without speaking. George dried in tandem with my scrubbing, but when I switched places, he lost his rhythm. If we stayed together long enough, I could grow old without George knowing. Just linger in his blind spot.

Later we crawled into bed with the tentativeness of new lovers. I flicked off the switch before George settled beneath my comforter. Now he felt more like an unwanted guest, the eye changing everything. I used to tell George the kind of bedtime stories that eased his body into mine, how I was so happy to show off my stencil of flowers blooming across the walls, how I embroidered the edges of my comforter with the same cheerful petals all those nights when I stayed home alone.

But I was never really alone. Men have crawled in and out of my bed since I was a teenager, but none of them bothered spending enough time to notice me. To George I wove my bedroom into a secret clubhouse with a combination only he could decode. Men love feeling like they can show you all those things you've never learned. They want you to be clumsy. They want you to need their help. They want you to admire them, even when they fumble with your buttons and need to be guided into you. Now, in the dark, I heard a different kind of fumbling. Almost imperceptible, as I strained towards George, I heard a faint pop like the sound of an apple being plucked off a tree. George turned over. The glass eye rolled around on the end table with the anticipation that only comes when there is nowhere to go.

I asked, "Don't you have to keep it in water?" as I stretched out my nightgown to tuck my cold feet into its flannel hem.

"It's not dentures."

"But I haven't dusted in weeks. Aren't you afraid of germs?"

"Once you lose an eye, you stop sweating the small stuff. I worry more about my ocular prosthesis breaking. That's why I always travel with an extra. I keep it in a pouch next to my toothbrush."

"You do?"

"It's not as bad as you think. I mean, artificial eyes have been around since the fifth century B.C. The first ones were made of clay, and people actually wore them outside the eye socket."

My feet refused to warm up. I slowly untucked my toes and touched them to George's ankles. "You sure know a lot about this."

"It gets even better. They made the first in-socket eyes out of gold. Think how rich I'd look if they still did that today?"

When I finally asked, "Does it hurt getting it in and out?" George answered me with a snore. I turned over and thought about how the optometrist always pushes me to get contacts, and how I always fail the test. Dr. Rogers refuses to order the lenses until I can touch my eyeball. And she doesn't even have a sink in her office where I can wash my hands first.

George sank into a deeper sleep. From the end table came the sound of something lingering in the dark. Awake. Always awake. A peeping Tom, if such a thing could be formed of glass, watched me trying to slip into any dream that would elude its constant stare. An eye, glass or not, without its accoutrements—the lid, lashes, brow—becomes all-knowing, void of any emotion except that insouciant sense that nothing slips by it. I tossed and I turned. I fluffed my pillow. I changed from a flannel nightgown to silk pajamas back to the flannel. It kept watching. The eye saw me in a way I never dared to imagine. A conjurer of every woman's dream, I could hold onto its attention for an eternity. My breasts could fall, my hair thin, that moustache above my lip grow and thicken, but the eye would never look away.

In the morning my actions let George assume I had accepted his defect. I even celebrated the weekday morning with pancakes fluffed in butter. By dinnertime, another day behind us like a torn calendar page, we reclaimed our nightly routine of reading the newspaper, cooking dinner together, me pretending to listen while George detailed his afternoon of grinding lenses.

After dinner I rushed into bed with a headache. Beside me George read a biography of some general from World War II. When he drifted so far into sleep the tome slid from his lap, I turned to see the eye illuminated under a reading lamp on the edge of the end table. Reaching across George's body, I grasped the glass in my hand. The eye was already cold. First, it warmed when I breathed into my palm. Did the eye's pupil dilate under the moist perimeters of my skin?

On the next exhale of George's most vociferous snore, I touched the eye to me. Nothing ever felt as sure as the convex disc skimming my flannel nightgown to rub the woman beneath.

With my own eyes closed I plunged the prosthetic deep into my body. It wasn't erotic, or even medical, but philosophical the way the smooth stone contemplated my being. I was becoming more real than I'd ever been. A gift I would never give up.

Even crawling out of bed brought pleasure, for no one invisible could be so illicit. I stashed George's eye in the pocket of my nightgown. In the bathroom, I burgled my way through his toiletries to abscond with his back-up lens. I had no intention of leaving forever. Everyone knows that escape doesn't work that way. As soon as you settle into the next town, the next house, the next bed, that becomes the next place you long to leave. The eyes and I just went joy riding.

Night closed in all around us, me in my flannel with my two glass-eyed companions arranged on the car dashboard for the best view.

We wound down the bluffs past the center of town. I took over as tour director, showing the two glass eyes where I bought my groceries, which dry cleaner always removed every spot, who made the best coffee. The eyes made quiet tourists, but how could they complain without mouths? We developed a kinship, the woman with no body and the eyes with no face. I told them I would gladly insert at least one of them into my own face if I knew how.

We curved around the bluffs and back towards my house as dawn blued the horizon. I was in no hurry, content knowing that I could dole out my lifetime of anecdotes in the coming nights. And George would never need to know.

The road became steeper at the base of my subdivision, a quick turn onto the gravel dislodging one of my glass passengers from its perch. I squirreled a hand along the floor mats, then kept one hand on the steering wheel while I ducked to scour the area around my feet for George's wandering eye.

When I sat back up, George was in the middle of the road waving his arms. His pajamas stuck to the sweat of his body. I could tell he was stumbling. With one eye closed he yelled at me in a voice so faint, it sounded like George was disappearing with the coming sun.

The closer George shuffled his slippered feet towards the center of the road, the more I imagined ether overtaking his body. There was nothing left to do but close both of my eyes and drive straight into a brand new morning, the two glass eyes my new navigators as I hoped the way they made me hit George with my car was only an optical illusion.

It was nice to be seen, even for a little while. And now I had a new set of eyes fixated on me, never even letting me down to blink.

INSPIRATIONAL WINNER

ON KISSING AGAIN WITH TEARS

Bradley J. Gustafson
Scottsbluff, NE

By any world measure, it was such a small and insignificant gift. I found a small black-and-white photograph in one of my great aunt Ollie's cardboard shoeboxes, pausing only momentarily before slipping the American gothic image surreptitiously into my pocket. It took me a week to find someone to write out the short Tennyson poem in calligraphy. A girl at the framing shop matted the poem and the photo separately within the boundaries of one burgundy frame. Then late one September afternoon Dad and I drove over to her rented duplex apartment to give the picture back her life as I saw it—blown up, framed and named, and neatly wrapped in butcher's paper.

Garrison Keillor likes to say there are two kinds of Swedes, Happy Swedes and Dark Swedes. Members of my own family who have known me in my brooding hours would vouch for my being definitely of the congenital Dark Swede variety, and they're not talking about my brown hair and hazel eyes. I have learned how to periodically make people smile, but only because I know what makes them sad.

Born in 1895, Ollie was 92 and failing that brown autumn afternoon, with only a mile or two, six months or so, before her sleep. As my father parked the pickup beneath the shade of the dying elm trees, I cradled the gift in my lap. Dad walked with me up the concrete steps to her stoop, where her smile pushed open the screen door to greet us.

The photograph had been taken sometime in the 1930s, and shows Ollie standing next to two tired and harnessed mules. She smiles into the camera, motionless below the barn's elevated haymow door. Above and just behind her atop the grain wagon's sideboard sits her beloved husband, Eric, who hunches slightly forward as he fails to muster a smile. He is obviously fatigued from a long day in the fields, his overalls and leather gloves dusty, his face weathered in the sun.

My single thought as I handed Ollie the package and invited her to sit down with us on her sofa was this: that nestled at the heart of love lie not common sentiments but common wounds. In the depressions of our own thirties, we are not always privy to the contours of our own wounds. Yet somehow I had always been aware of hers, my fledgling farm boy's soul having been nourished beneath the canopy of her grief.

Awash and adrift in a relentless sea of Nebraska corn, my nuclear family of five survived and ultimately thrived on a well-stocked island of chicken coops and granaries. Our barn was always busy with hay and milk, our gardened pantry stacked high with the staples of love.

Yet my first memories are not of our island but of theirs, that enchanted acre of mournful mirth half a mile away, where for almost four decades together Eric and Ollie harvested corn, milked cows, fed dogs, raised vegetables, butchered chickens, percolated coffee and entertained wandering relatives. It was, we all remembered, to their island I instinctively walked as a five-year-old the day our gentle and all-knowing Dalmatian, Duke, died, treading as I did across the divide of our stubble-strewn cornfield as across the universal threshold of loss. By the time my trembling frame reached their mailbox, my fledgling soul was openly crying into the sky, searching for the solace of the ear that hears, the eye that sees.

Why does the grown boy remember with love and gratitude all these decades later, the simple sight of Ollie lifting her eyes above the sill of the washhouse window, and the simple act of Eric gently sliding his thin frame out from beneath a grain truck in their graveled yard to ask the grieving boy, What's the matter? Is it not remembered because that was all the boy needed in that dark and dreary hour?

Is it not because that is all anyone needs in such an hour: someone to simply hear and see that my evaporating innocence sought the cover of mercy where it could most readily be found, in furrows already chiseled by the merciless blades of grief? And as any six-year-old boy could see, a grief of Biblical proportions lived in both of their eyes.

By any world measure, the death of their boy had been such a small and insignificant death. He had not lived long enough to be given even a name. His small stone in the hilltop graveyard above my Nebraska hometown reads simply, A Son, and the date on which he was stillborn in the year of our Lord, 1928. Thirty-three years old when she suffered this fateful pregnancy, the doctor had told Ollie in the depths of her labor that this would be her only child. A minister visited, neighbors brought meals, a short religious service was hastily arranged in the churchyard four miles away with a silent vigil of family standing near. Then the death became nothing but one more tragic miscarriage of hope swept beneath the carpet of time.

Years later, she gave me the uniform Eric had worn in the trenches of France, complete with gas mask, leggings and a captured lighter with Gott mit uns engraved on its side. Fighting with General Jack Pershing's American Expeditionary Force in the last months of 1918, Eric had been gassed by a mustard cloud and left for dead in a muddy field. He lay for hours until a horse-drawn cart of a death-detail passed by a second time. Some unnamed soldier saw him take a breath and said, O what the hell, and threw him on just in case he'd pull through. An older relative told me once that war had softened Eric in all the right ways. He was a man who had seen the river of life and death overflowing the war-strewn banks of the world, and part of it had become lodged there, too, you could see it, in his sad, rural Nebraska eyes.

And so it was after the war and after the miscarriage that my Great Uncle Eric and Aunt Ollie had settled into their life together without children, surrounded by siblings and neighbors, mules and barns. And relatives.

No one had more community-wide birthday parties at her home than Ollie did; no one served more coffee at later hours. Driving home through the darkened landscape, returning home from church or a late-night check of the fields, my father would always look out across the fields for her yard-light. The rule was, if the light was on, so was the coffee. And we would always stop by.

As a boy, what I remember are the little things that were huge. Like being asked by Ollie to mow her yard and always being welcome in her refrigerator. She and I played circus in her barn, with horse blankets draped over the sawhorses to look like bears. She let me swim in her livestock tank and sat beside me to let me drive her car down three country miles as far as the church. I can still smell with remarkable acuity both her incomparable cinnamon rolls in the afternoon, and the dusty jackets of the two devotionals she read from before we left the table each morning after breakfast. When she tucked me in for the night in my own bedroom upstairs in her cold and drafty attic floor, I fell into an eternal reverie with the rhythms of her antique clock, ticking away the hours and the years.

I still think these many years later, rightly or wrongly, that I was the most special among all her relation to her, perhaps the greatest tribute to her adoptive skills. The role she came throughout her life to play for me was no less than that of a full-fledged grandmother, even long after that cold day in 1960 when Eric's war-wounded lungs and heart finally gave out in spite of forty years of fresh air, and he slumped over in the yard one fall afternoon during corn-picking season and died, with Ollie and dinner waiting on him in the house.

And so it was decades later, a short six months before she died, with her heart still full of that peculiar love that has been drenched in tears, I decided on a long-percolating whim to give Ollie my gift. It was the only present I could muster. In my own early thirties by this time, unmarried and childless with not much sense of my own future, I had this acute sensibility concerning her past, a past I also now knew was an interwoven thread in the fabric of my own.

She opened the package, but began to cry and could not read the poem. She handed it to my father, who after a moment passed it to me. The poem was Tennyson's "As Through The Land At Eve We Went," and I read it for all of us, aloud.

As through the land at eve we went
And plucked the ripened ears
We fell out, my wife and I
O, we fell out I know not why
And kissed again with tears.
And blessings on the falling out

That all the more endears
When we fall out with those we love
And kiss again with tears!
For when we came, where lies the child
We lost in other years
There above the little grave
O, there above the little grave
We kissed again with tears.

By the time the poem was finished, Ollie was weeping; my dad was weeping; I was weeping. Yet, rarely if ever have I been in a room filled with more genuine joy. It was the joy at being known and seen, the joy of being connected by love to the world, the joy of a grief observed and acknowledged and somehow, miraculously, redeemed.

I do not remember so much my Aunt Ollie's tears that day. What I will always remember is the unconscious and sudden joy with which she suddenly leapt up and ran to the door, pushed open the screen, and yelled for her neighbor to come. Her neighbor was working in his yard, old Mr. Higby; tall and soft-spoken, he was the retired town funeral director. Come and see, she hollered to him. What is it? I heard quiet Mr. Higby ask. The man who had buried Eric thirty years before, and so many others of her loved ones, leaned his rake against the wall of his home. What is it?, he said again.

All she could muster as she stood in the doorway, waiting for him to come was, O come, see!

MAINSTREAM/LITERARY SHORT STORY WINNER

NOTHING AT ALL IS MORE THAN ENOUGH

Jeff McCormick
Lakeland, FL

The south side of Tampa reminds me of an old dog's belly, sagging, clumps of fur fallen away, visible veins—a river, railroad tracks, highways, tangles of narrow side roads.

Exhalations from a fertilizer factory often make the air smell like burnt chocolate-chip cookies.

East of U.S. 41, hugging the river, there's a little trailer park. Mostly rentals. I moved in about a month ago.

I'm almost certain no one who knows me would think to seek me out here. And that's a good thing. Hell, even I can't believe I'm hiding here.

It's the first week of June.

My new home is a rented brown-and-white trailer, furnished, near the back of the park, close to a bend in the river. Water oaks twist like arthritic fingers over the aluminum rectangles. Shading them, encouraging algae to grow up the sides. The cars parked in the driveways off the one-lane, one-way loop of road are older, with mismatched tires and coats of grime. They're parked outside because most of the carports have been screened to become porches. My battered Cavalier fits right in.

The park is quiet most of the time.

There's another fugitive living here. He's about my age. Fifty. I know he's hiding from something because he looks at me sideways at first and then with a smirk that seems to say: You, too, huh?

Most of the neighbors are white haired and private. In the early evenings, their televisions fill the park with game-show noise—shouting, laughter and applause. By ten o'clock, all's quiet.

A few trailers to the west lives a younger woman, maybe in her late thirties. She's thin, and has a black-and-white collie that she walks in the morning and just before dark. I say hello if I see her, but she only nods and does not speak or smile. Her face is not pretty, but her black hair is.

A younger man and woman live across from her. The man leaves for work at night. He looks like Martin Luther King Jr. Walks with a limp. She is tall and attractive, skin like wet coal, always wears bright blouses.

The only neighbor who has come over to introduce herself is Nellie Bunning.

She's about five feet tall, has hair like a snowdrift, a face full of wrinkles and walks stooped behind a walker. She lives two trailers to the east of me and

27

on the other side of the lane.

It's the second week of June.

The other fugitive and I see each other for the third time the afternoon a diamondback crosses the lane. Nellie sees it. Her screams wake me from a nap on the sofa on my screened porch. I bolt out the door, certain that they've found me and I need to run. Then I see Nellie, and she points at the pavement in front of her place.

The snake glides across the lane like a toy train, away from Nellie, who has stopped screaming. Sunlight filtering through the oaks makes the brown-and-tan rattler glitter. It's almost as long as the one-lane road is wide and about three inches thick. It keeps its body straight, its rattles up, its ribs rippling against its scales as it propels itself. Then disappearing into the palmettos and oaks that wall off the river.

"Oh, my God!" Nellie cries and raises her swollen wrist to her forehead. "That terrible thing must live right here!"

"It's just passing through," I tell her, trying to sound like an expert.

"You need to kill it!" Nellie leans on her walker, pulls it closer to her wide hips. Her ankles, protruding under orange slacks, are puffy and purple. "I want you to kill it! You've got to!"

I don't say anything. I see the other fugitive, and our eyes meet for a moment, and he gives me that "You, too?" look.

He's got a boy living with him. Tall, skinny kid. Maybe twelve, maybe fifteen. I assume it's his son, though they don't look much alike. Maybe a nephew.

Nellie shouts: "Did you hear me?"

I shake my head and go inside.

Other than the diamondback incident, the park stays quiet. I like that. No one plays music loud late at night. No yelling. After the televisions are shut off, there's only the hum and roar from the highway, punctuated by the rumble and horn blasts of the trains.

The place has many good sounds. The breeze hums in the trees. Tree frogs and crickets sing at night. Cicadas buzz in the treetops. A pair of whippoorwills whistle down along the riverbank. Mockingbirds and woodpeckers chatter in the mornings.

Most of the park's residents are retired, but many of the younger people work during the day. Some of them work at night.

I wonder what they think of me, young enough to have a job and strong, but not working. And still having money to spend on groceries and gas for the Cavalier.

I wonder about myself, too. Do I really need to do this? To hide out like this? I guess I do. It's the first time in more than a year I've slept well.

Still, I have to shake my head. At this point in my life. Living only one step up from being a bum. A downward spiral. Into a shady slum. After my life had had such a great start. Now always looking over my shoulder. But it is exciting.

I wonder about the other fugitive. He doesn't work either. He stays in his trailer most of the time. The boy, when he does step outside, is whiter than a fish belly. Not natural for a kid in Florida. And he's never outdoors without the man.

It's the third week of June.

Florida's rainy season starts.

Next door to me, Curt Olsen keeps his trailer door open most of the time. We introduced ourselves a few days ago at the mailbox. I can hear his television. If I look between trees, I can see him sitting with his feet up in his recliner. White T-shirt. Big belly. Bald head with white fringe over his ears. Yesterday, he was on his porch and saw me, and invited me over for a beer.

He's retired from Chrysler. "Forty years on the line!" he boasts. He's full of questions about where I'm from and what line of work I'm in. I'm evasive. Almost rude. I figure I won't get asked back. We drink Miller. It tastes good on a warm afternoon. He stops with the questions. He talks. He considers himself a philosopher. Has many interesting, if impractical ideas about world peace. His deep voice sounds like little stones tumbling over bigger stones.

"What was it like where you come from?" Curt asks, again prying.

"Quiet," I tell him, avoiding where he wants the conversation to go.

He pries about family. But I don't tell him anything.

When he yawns, I finish my beer and thank him and go back to my little home.

I spend most of my time on my porch, reading some, staring out through the screen more, watching the narrow lane, listening. Wondering if they'll find me here. Will I have sense enough to leave first? Sometimes sirens out on the highway make me nervous. Or strange cars rolling down the park's narrow lane.

It's the fourth week of June.

The thunderstorms arrive from the east in the late afternoon and end about sunset. They make the trailer park seem like a jungle encampment. Curtains of rain hiss through the trees. Lightning zips among the branches. Thunder shakes the ground.

There's a bar and restaurant about a mile north of the park. I go there on Friday and Saturday nights. I can't be a hermit all the time.

The place is called Slinger's. Good, greasy cheeseburgers and cold beer. The music and voices are loud. During and after the rainstorms, two buckets sit under where the roof leaks, and water drips in sturdy plops.

On Friday, I'm sitting in the bar after dinner, nursing my last beer, putting off going home, when the woman who walks the collie comes in. She sits at the other end of the bar.

She sees me and smiles. Nods.

I smile and nod back.

She looks at the empty barstool beside her, then at me. Raises her eyebrows. They are thick, black eyebrows.

I take the hint and carry my beer over to sit beside her.

From across the room, she looks almost attractive. The illusion disappears at close range. But her hair is lush and gleaming. It smells nice, too. Like jasmine.

"Hello, neighbor," I say.

She smiles. "Hi."

A nice smile. Full, pale lips.

I tell her my new name.

"Hello, Noah Morgan." She holds out her narrow hand. I shake it. Cool skin and long, bony fingers.

She says, "Ann Frazier."

"Nice to meet you, Ann. How's your dog?"

"Barney? Oh, he's great! He's my best bud."

"He's a nice-looking dog." I wish I could compliment her.

"I know. He's a beauty." Ann has a New York accent.

We sip our beers.

Ann says, "You're the mystery man of the trailer park, ya know."

"I am?"

"Yeah! For sure! Everyone wonders who you are, where you came from and why you're there. But Nellie's mad at you."

I laugh. "Why?"

"Because you wouldn't kill that rattler."

"It didn't need killing. It's probably keeping the rat population under control."

"You're a nature lover, huh?" She says it like an insult. But grins.

"Yeah. I'm a nature lover." I drink from my beer and look straight ahead.

"Me, too. But poisonous reptiles make me nervous."

"As they should. Just leave them alone, and chances are they'll leave you alone."

"I worry about my dog."

"Yeah. That could be a problem. But I don't think the rattler is a permanent resident. Unless our little park has a lot of rats."

"Only the two-legged kind."

I look at her and raise my eyebrows.

She raises her eyebrows at me in reply. They are sexy eyebrows. I wonder if I'm getting drunk or I've just been alone for too long.

"So," she says, "who are you, Noah Morgan?"

"I want to know more about the rats."

She shakes her head. "You'll find out. I hope you're not gonna turn out to be one of 'em." She takes off her rain jacket. A sleeveless and low-cut blouse underneath. As she twists around to hang the jacket on the back of her chair, I glance down the front of her blouse. I like what I see.

She puts her pencil-thin arms on the bar. Rows of black hairs and a few freckles from her elbows to her wrists.

"So? Who or what is Noah Morgan?"

"I'm me. I'm retired. I'm looking for quiet."

Ann studies my face. I don't find her as homely as I did a few minutes ago. But I feel like I'm too old for her.

"You don't look old enough to be retired."

I smile because of what I had just been thinking. "I got lucky. So what do you do?"

She shrugs. "I work at Riverside Industrial Lift over on 301."

I've noticed the place. They sell forklifts and other industrial equipment. Her hands are nice, so I assume she works in the office.

She finishes her beer, puts the glass at the edge of the bar and nods to the bartender that she wants another.

I'm near my limit, so I sip mine.

The bartender serves Ann. He looks at me. I shake my head.

Ann grins, takes a long drink from her glass. Licks the foam from her upper lip.

Thunder overhead.

"Looks like a rainy night," Ann says.

"How long have you lived in Florida?"

She turns toward me and raises her chin. Looks at me with half-shut eyes. "Ten years, about. Why?"

"Just curious. Do you ever go back to New York?"

She smiles. "Accent's that obvious, huh?" She sips her beer, makes a face as if it tastes bitter. "Not for a long time. Where you from?"

I lie, but tell her a neighboring state in case she knows accents.

"Never been there."

We sip and probe about spouses, relationships and baggage. We're both divorced. Kids elsewhere. Then we don't talk for a while. She nods her head in time with the music. We talk about songs and bands we like. Then are quiet again.

She starts to take another sip, but puts the half-full glass down. "I've gotta go."

I'm surprised.

She has her jacket on and is off the stool before I can say anything.

"Goodnight," she says.

"Goodnight."

And she's gone.

It's the first week of July.

Ann looks at my trailer when she and her dog walk past. She waves. I invite her out to dinner. She accepts. We go to a nice restaurant in Tampa. Still curious, she asks more questions about me. But I stay vague with my answers. Annoyed, she stops asking. Says little on the way home. A quick kiss goodnight on her top step.

I think the man who looks like Martin Luther King has lost his job. He stays home a lot.

We say hello, but we've never introduced ourselves.

Summer gets hotter. The trailers' air conditioners hum all day and all night.

Ann hasn't been around for a few days.

I sit on my porch and watch a lizard climb the screen. It grabs a brown spider in its jaws and chomps it and swallows it. I think that it's a rotten world where animals have to eat each other.

On Friday night, I come home from Slinger's about ten o'clock. I've made some friends there, but I'm careful that no one knows me too well. Or where I live.

It's a dark night. The stars seem to be even farther away, and heat lightning dances behind a mountain of clouds to the south.

Most of the televisions have been turned off. A train rumbles across U.S. 41, its bell dinging.

I sit on my porch, thinking and watching the night.

A shadow crosses my small front yard. "Hey, Noah. You in there?" Ann's voice.

"Yeah."

She comes to the screen.

The breeze carries her perfume to me. I can smell her better than I can see her.

"What's up?" I ask, hoping she wants some company.

"There were a couple of guys snooping around your place just after sunset." My heart hangs in mid-beat, then goes bouncing, making me so dizzy I almost fall over.

I cough, and Ann asks, "Are you all right?"

"Yeah."

"You could invite me in."

I want to be throwing clothes into my suitcase, but I open the door. I need to know for sure before I run.

She comes in. "Whatcha sittin' in the dark for?"

"Just listening to the night."

"Ah. Okay. You got any beer?"

I'm shaking, and I'm glad it's dark.

"Yup. You want a glass?"

"Nope. Bottle is fine."

When I return, I hand the bottle to her. I've got one for myself. She sits in my chair. I sit on the sofa. It squeaks when I lean back.

"I haven't seen you around lately," I say.

"I've been working a lot of overtime. Going in early, staying late."

I think I should apologize for the other night. But it's too late now, because I'll be leaving in the morning, and I don't say anything. I'm still wondering why she's here. In the dark. Wearing nice perfume.

I can almost see her face. She raises the bottle to her lips.

Awkward silence. I want to ask about the two men, but don't know how. Tree frogs in the oaks chirp. An owl hoots. The breeze cools the sweat on my forehead.

Ann says, "So, why would two guys be poking around here?"

"I don't know."

She exhales like a snort. Not believing me.

She says, "Are you ever going to tell me what you're doing here? You're not the typical person who lives in a trailer park."

"Hey, you live here and seem to like it. Besides, I thought I told you about that."

"I live here because I'm broke. But you've sidestepped the issue. Twice. Then tonight, those guys were poking around here and at that other guy's trailer. The guy with the kid. What's up with you?"

I'm glad Ann can't see my fear. It takes me a moment to be able to talk without my voice shaking. I cough. Then: "Who were they?"

"How should I know? I came home from work, and I saw them when I was unloading groceries."

"What'd they look like?"

"I couldn't see that well. It was almost night. They wore dark clothes."

"There were two of 'em." I know I sound inane.

"Yeah. Two. One taller than the other."

I taste something sour at the back of my throat. "Did they come inside my place?"

"I don't think so. I watched 'em. They drove down to the other guy's trailer. Walked all the way around it. Then drove away. I guess he and the kid weren't home either."

"What kind of car?"

"Big. Blue or black. Lincoln, maybe."

Sweat is running down my back. I'm tempted to charge out the door, hop into my Cavalier and go. But something tells me: Not yet.

"Who you running from?" Ann asks. "The law?"

"It's not that simple."

Ann sits beside me on the sofa. I jump when she touches my wrist.

"Hey," she coos. "I really like dangerous men." Laughs.

I laugh. "I'm not dangerous."

My mind is racing. Do I need to pack and leave?

Ann touches me again. I don't jump. She nuzzles. We kiss.

I wonder: What's this all about? A trap?

She whispers, "I wanted us to do this the other night. Ya know?"

"Me, too."

After awhile, we're lying down. The scent under her arms reminds me of a candy I liked when I was a boy.

In the morning, before dawn, she has gone. But her perfume still fills the trailer. The bedroom is a wreck—pillows and a sheet on the floor.

As the sun rises, I'm drinking orange juice on the porch when Ann in T-shirt and shorts walks by with her dog. She grins at me and keeps walking, with her thin legs pale in the early light.

Everything is dewy, twinkling in the sun's horizontal rays.

While eating a small breakfast, I start packing. I should have left last night, I think. But that would've raised suspicions, another voice in my head argues.

I hear a car coming. I sidestep to the porch and paste myself against the wall to peek outside.

Too late now! a thought teases.

A dark-blue Crown Victoria glides past. Stops in front of the other fugitive's trailer. A white-and-green sheriff's cruiser knifes through the shadows, stops behind the Crown Vic.

All four cops get out. Two in uniform, one of them a woman, and two men in suits. All with bulletproof vests. They leave the cars' engines running.

The sun's in my eyes. It's hard to see.

An officer bangs on the trailer door. Steps away. Curt and Nellie stand in their driveways, watching. I peek around the corner. Ann is out. And the man and woman across the lane.

The fugitive opens his door, and the two cops in suits rush up and push their way in. The uniformed deputies stay outside, hands on their holsters.

My brain is dancing, laughing. Those cops could be famous if they knew I was here.

Newspapers across Florida and in St. Louis and Chicago would have big headlines if they were arresting me instead of him. But I'm safe. For now.

The boy shuffles out of the trailer. The female deputy takes his arm. I think the boy is crying. The sun is still low, and they are in shadow. She helps him get into the back of the cruiser.

The two officers in suits march out with the man between them, holding his arms. They are shouting, telling him his rights.

He is in handcuffs, and they put him in the back of the Crown Vic. Car doors slam.

Engines rev, and the cars glide down the lane. I can hear them making the loop and going out to the highway on the other side of the park. Two minutes later, a TV news van pulls up, and the reporter stands in front of the trailer, pushing her hair out of her face as she talks to the camera. And we neighbors learn the story.

The man had kidnapped the boy four years ago in Pennsylvania and moved to Florida, living in three different cities before being tracked down in our little park.

The reporter keeps stumbling over words and names. It takes her five tries to get the story on film. I wonder if she has it correct even then. The TV crew drives away.

After a few minutes, the birds start singing again.

Another TV news crew shows up. A male reporter. Handsome, but he needs at least ten tries to film his report without flubbing it.

Afterward, several of the neighbors stand in the lane and talk. I can hear them saying how shocked they are. I'm not shocked. I'm disappointed for seeing it and knowing it, and not admitting I knew what it was. I shake my head at myself for thinking that that guy, that piece of crud, and me had something in common. We were just hiding out. And there's nothing unusual about that.

I remember Ann telling me that I'd been the topic of conversation throughout the park. I get uneasy again. Convince myself to finish packing and move on. Sad. Because I like this place.

I put my packed bags in the closet, then sit on the porch. I'll load the car after dark and head out. Where? I ask myself. Shrug. Sure don't know. North, I guess. Not much choice.

Ann and her dog come up to the screen, and she says, "Did you see all the excitement?"

"Yeah."

"Isn't that something? Right here in our little park?"

"Yeah. A real surprise."

"What secrets some people have, huh?"

"Makes you wonder."

"For sure." She and the dog continue their walk.

During the afternoon rain, I fall asleep on the sofa. A dream about Crown Victorias coming down the lane wakes me. The sun is setting. I'm hungry.

Curt is talking to Nellie. Nellie glances toward my trailer. I hope she can't see me behind the screen. I think I'm the topic of their conversation. Will the police come for me next?

The sun is shining behind the oak branches. Thick bands of gold light streak through.

I change my mind about leaving. Then change it about staying. Sometimes I think I'm the dumbest son of a bitch on the planet and it's a miracle I'm still alive. This is one of those times. I convince myself to stay, reasoning that leaving will draw attention to me. Ann, Nellie and the others would suspect something. Everything is packed, so I can leave quickly if I get a whiff of trouble. I smile, knowing that's stupid. But I stay. Fix supper.

Ann comes over after dark.

It's the second week of July.

It's the third week of July.

The air smells like burnt cookies. Summer's heat hangs heavy, even in the shade. The cicadas drone all day.

The trailer where the man and boy lived stays empty. Shunned.

Ann's visits taper off. She gives no reason. Maybe I'm no longer dangerous.

My birthday was yesterday. There's more years behind me than I've got ahead. A thought that makes me uneasy.

I'll be leaving this trailer park soon.

But today still isn't the day.

MEMOIR/PERSONAL ESSAY WINNER

DISABILITY AND THE DESIRE FOR LOVE
Todd Gauchat, with Deborah Burke
Lakewood, OH

"Would you like to see my breast?" asked the thin girl with long brown hair sitting on the bench beside me. Rosalind and I had been having long talks, taken walks in the woods; we'd become friends. She made me laugh. Now, here she was, a soft smile on her face, offering me the intimacy my heart had longed for. I was desperately missing this part of life. I was twenty-nine years old and severely disabled since birth by cerebral palsy. I had been rejected too many times as a lover.

I looked at Rosalind, nodded *yes*, once, twice, three times. She slipped a small creamy breast out of her dress. I leaned forward in my wheelchair, not wanting to miss a second of this incredible gift. This was what life was about, just this—a woman's breast. Rosalind smiled and then quickly tucked it away. I lowered myself to the ground, hoping she would get my drift. The ground was hard and bumpy under the huge spruce surrounded by wild violets. Rosalind slid off the bench and lay next to me.

Suddenly, my left arm—the only arm that has ever worked—began flailing around. I have no control over my body's spastic movements. I'm lucky I didn't accidentally knock Rosalind unconscious.

I reached out to her. We kissed. She didn't seem to mind my head-shaking, drippy kisses. Rosalind slid her breast out and I tried to touch it, but my arm wouldn't cooperate. We gazed into each other's eyes.

***

I have a whole list of impossibles: I can't feed myself, drive a car, or walk. I can't wipe my own butt or brush my teeth. I can't talk except to form letters with my mouth, point them out on a letter-board, or have an assistive device speak for me in digitally synthesized monotone.

As a teen, I had a one-track mind: I wanted to find love more than I wanted to walk. I don't believe that any of us—well-bodied or disabled—can circumvent the need for intimacy. It's critical to our physical, emotional and, in a real sense, spiritual maturity.

Yet, well-meaning folks discouraged me from believing love was possible. They seemed surprised that I even had sexual longings, that because my body was disabled, my feelings of passion were also disabled. Turned off. Disconnected.

As a teen, this hunger for passion and intimacy tormented me. After all, girls in my classes weren't exactly asking to sit on my lap for a wheelchair ride to their lockers. A question began burning deep within me, and I reduced it to its essence. I asked friends, family, and teachers: "WHAT ARE MY CHANCES FOR SEX AND MARRIAGE?"

People stood behind my wheelchair, spelling the words aloud as I pointed to each letter on a letter-board on my lap. When "sex" came up, people sighed and said, "Oh, Todd," as if my question was sadly ridiculous. I've heard so much discouragement that I could have packaged it and sold it as fertilizer. Here's a sampling:

"Todd, girls are a picky bunch."

"Forget sex. It's not all it's cracked up to be."

"Todd, you can't make love to a woman because you can't lie on top of her."

"It's not going to happen, Todd."

But I was obsessed with desire.

When I put my question to a friendly girl in class, she responded, "I hope I don't hurt your feelings, Todd. I think you're a great guy and I really value your friendship. Now don't be mad! But I don't think that dream is possible for you."

I wasn't mad. I was determined. It's been a long, painful journey.

***

I didn't fit the ideal image of a boyfriend. Girls saw only my body's contorted and spastic movements, my inability to talk or walk. How could they know there was a deeply passionate man inside? Yet, passion doesn't originate in the body but in the spirit, the soul, the deepest part of our self. Sexuality is deep energy and imagination; it has nothing to do with the body's condition. My body is disabled but must it follow that my soul is disabled, my sexuality, my passion, or my creativity? I am as passionate as my well-bodied friends.

Even my adoptive mother—so often my champion— told me I had to be "realistic" about love. How many dreams—at their core—are realistic? Imagination, creativity, love, passion—not one of these profound experiences is realistic. That's why they're profound—and necessary.

I was shy and afraid of rejection. I pursued girls in my mind more than by wheelchair. When a girl was friendly, I'd ask her to become my girlfriend. I became deeply depressed when not one would even consider it.

In my twenties, I wanted a relationship that would lead to marriage, but women wanted only friendship, unsure of how sex would work. If they'd asked, I would have suggested we experiment, figure it out as we went along. If I hadn't known that I could perform the sexual act, I would never have been so single-minded. But women were too frightened to try—and maybe I was scared too.

I focused my attention during my early twenties on a woman who was a friend of the family. Mary and I would take off together to concerts by James Taylor or Peter, Paul and Mary. I developed a serious crush on Mary and told her. She quickly confronted me.

"I am not interested in becoming your lover," she said. She knew what I wanted.

When Mary left for New York, my feelings for her deepened. I wrote her long love letters on a typewriter, unbelievably certain she would return my love. The bubble of happiness burst big.

One day when a letter from Mary arrived, I went to my room to be alone. I transferred myself from my wheelchair to the bed, turned on the radio, and eagerly opened the letter.

"I received your letters, Todd, and I am amazed and angered that you are still pursuing this dead-end path of love for me. They must stop. I am not in love with you."

I fought against the fear lurking at the edges of my awareness that I was being rejected again. Minnie Riverton's "Loving You" came on the radio; I started to cry. I was wounded to the core of my being and decided to end my life. The decision came quickly and without argument.

I lowered myself to the floor, next to the radio where I also kept a basin of water and a washcloth. I placed the radio on my lap and the soaking washcloth on the radio and waited to be electrocuted. For two hours I tried —but there wasn't even a crackle. Why the hell can't I kill myself? I cried. It seems now like a simple—even ridiculous—plan, but my options for suicide were severely limited, like my chances for love.

On the wall in my bedroom hung a crucifix. I felt nailed— to the crosses of disability and rejection. I wanted so much to be set free from the pain of both crosses. This was the darkest moment of my life.

Today, I see that the darkness held blessings. Those rejections made me grow up. I stopped obsessing about sex. I no longer misinterpreted friendliness as sexual interest. I created a shell around my interactions with women, learning to protect myself. I never again wanted to be depressed enough to lose trust in the God of Mercy and end my life. Those dark moments carved me into a more mature person. I am grateful I couldn't end my life. Had I been successful, I would have missed the best part. I didn't know that dark day that one thin, sexy, able-bodied woman with a great sense of humor would come into my life and pursue me.

***

Until I met Rosalind, my experience had been that people felt uncomfortable around me. But Rosalind put me at ease. She didn't patronize me as if I were a child or hard of hearing. She didn't feel sorry for me, tiptoe around my feelings, or let me off any hook just because I had a disability. She didn't become restless when I asked slow-going questions on the letter-board. She spoke her mind, which helped me understand and speak my own. Rosalind was the first to confirm that I was a normal guy—something I longed to be.

After talking in the garden for months, Rosalind and I kissed. We petted. We didn't have sex, but we spent a lot of time together. In summer 1985, I wanted time alone with Rosalind. We took Amtrak to Wisconsin to visit my cousin Rick. Rosalind begged Rick to take us in his canoe up the Monomonee

River to see eagles. Rick and Ros got me in the canoe and off we paddled. During a long day on a cool river; we saw plenty of nests but no eagles. By the time we returned to shore, I was—and felt—as stiff as a board. Yet, we had a great time. Rick smiled at us as if he knew a secret and we didn't.

Then one evening, as I waited for the sports scores during the evening news, Rosalind said, "I love you, Todd." I remember the flush of heat on my face and the small electric buzz that ran through every cell in my body. I remember I didn't believe her.

I knew my heart had never been happier, that I loved her too. But the crazy mind trolls started yapping: Rosalind doesn't love you, you fool. Not really. I looked hard at Rosalind. She nodded, confirming her words. Over the next few weeks, I asked Rosalind time and again if she really did love me. Always, she said yes.

***

Rosalind and I married in June 1986. We had no trouble working out the finer points of sex. I can't talk, so whispering sweet nothings was never part of our romance. I still had the use of my left arm and I could hold Rosalind, and hug her to me. I could say a few simple words back then but "sex" wasn't one of them. When the mood struck, I looked at Ros and said "rub"—our code word. We lay together, two naked, sensuous bodies, longing for each other, our souls listening to each other's heart beat. The intimacy I had craved was fully satisfied. The world over, sexual intimacy and love are just this simple—and necessary.

We wanted children but after a year of marriage Rosalind wasn't pregnant. The medical expert whose advice we sought said my disability would prevent me from impregnating my wife. Rosalind was devastated. She wept for days. Fortunately, like me, Ros won't take "no" for an answer. She researched medical books and came up with her own diagnosis: "Heat from your wheelchair seat is cooking your sperm, Todd," she said. "We have to cool you off!"

I didn't much like her plan, but I lived with it, blushing all the way. I knew Rosalind was born to be a mother. She cut a hole in my wheelchair seat and convinced me to go without underwear and let my gonads cool off. Nothing was noticeable or different when you looked at me in the wheelchair because Rosalind attached fabric to the wheelchair to keep her experiment private. Three months later she was pregnant; we have three sons.

In 2003, I contracted transverse myelitis, an inflammation of the spinal cord that has paralyzed me. Rosalind and I grieve the loss of sex, but intimacy continues. We have found that love can metamorphose into pure love that unites us in a far deeper way.

I am richly blessed. I would suffer the rejections and dark nights of the soul all over again to experience what I have had with Rosalind these last twenty-one years.

You might wonder, as I still do sometimes, why Rosalind loves me. All I know is that mystery abounds—especially in the impossible places of our amazing lives.

NON-RHYMING POETRY WINNER

THE QUILTS FROM GEE'S BEND, ALABAMA

Alison Luterman
Oakland, CA

Women who owned no shoes,
whose feet were hard as packed earth,
whose throats were open
flowers through which gospel poured,
made these praise-songs
of cotton, these shouts of necessary
color. In their work-
stiffened hands, the threaded needle,
shared scissors.
Here are the scraps
of a husband,
stained overalls, scorch
mark of denim punctuating the mute
expanse of fabric. Witness. Ripped
paisley tablecloth, shred of red scarf,
bleached fertilizer sacks.
Beauty's hours stolen
away from chopping and hoeing,
the cleaver, the bucket, and the well.
Testimony:
I like to hang my quilts all on a line
outside, and stand back till I see them wave
like flags from a long ways off,
a woman said, who learned
from her mother (who had sixteen
children, and not a shoe between them)
that if there was to be grace
in this life, she would have
to make it herself,
and that she could
and that it would live on.

RHYMING POETRY WINNER

THE ASIAN MARKET

James Anderson
North Miami, FL

Green tea and ginger flavors spice the air
between the crowded shelves packed tight with jars
of exotic sauce and pickled pears,
noodles, peppers, rice and vinegar.
The plastic Buddhas like to watch the show,
as shoppers gather herbs, and weigh the fish,
bag the beans and sprouts, find the miso
soup and gather items for their favorite dish.
The sound of wind chimes seems to resonate
with everyone who does their shopping there;
from every part of town they congregate,
from every race, from every class, from everywhere,
ingredients in a larger recipe
as they choose their apricots and tea.

STAGE PLAY WINNER

HUNGARIAN RHAPSODY: AN ELECTROGLIDE IN BLUE

Don Orwald
Granbury, TX

THE CAST:
WINGS: The desk sergeant, a heavy-set, kind man, in his 50s and in uniform
A GYPSY: Hard to tell her age, but maybe in her 40s and in full Gypsy regalia, headscarf, hoop earrings, the works
JULIE JONES: A slender, attractive, long-haired college student in a very colorful, revealing hippie dress
CAPTAIN IKE JONES: A very regular guy in his 40s or mid-50s, rumpled suit, shirt and tie

THE TIME: Spring of the mid-1970s

THE PLACE: New York City, a neighborhood police station

THE SET: Just left of center is the sergeant's desk with a chair behind it. A second chair is to stage right of the desk. Along the right wall and at an angle are a couple more chairs and a table with a coffee pot and cups. A soda machine is off stage right, the main entrance is down stage right. The captain enters from stage left.

AT RISE: The sergeant is at his desk doing paperwork and the gypsy enters, carrying a violin case. She speaks with a heavy middle European accent. She crosses to the desk's right corner. She puts the case on the desk and opens it.

GYPSY
I wan' to report a stolen violin.
SERGEANT
(Sees the violin.)
I don't understand. The violin is right here.
(Pause.)
Are you saying that you stole it and that now you are turning yourself in?
GYPSY
No, it was stolen by 'usban.

SERGEANT

Whose band?

GYPSY

Yes, my 'usban.

SERGEANT

(He's still confused until the GYPSY points to her wedding band.)
Oh your husband…he stole it?

(She nods yes.)

Where is he now?

GYPSY

In prison where he belong.

SERGEANT

I see…he stole your violin, he got locked up, you got it back. Sounds like justice to me.

GYPSY

No, not steal him from me. Steal from Ubermann.

SERGEANT

So, your husband is in jail for stealing a violin from a Mr. Hubert Mann?

GYPSY

No he in jail for stealing from aged women after marrying them.

SERGEANT

(Still confused.)

So your husband is a bigamist?

GYPSY

No, he's a bigga crook. He stole violin and then he play gypsy play.

SERGEANT

(Starting to run out of patience.)

So, your husband is a gypsy violin player and he stole this violin so he could play. Am I getting it right now?

GYPSY

Yes, he steal Ubermann's violin and this violin, he should go home now.

SERGEANT

(Picks up house phone.)

Let me call upstairs to my captain. I don't quite know how to handle this.
(JULIE enters, wearing bright hippie clothes and smoking a cigarette. She's a good kid, but is a bit rebellious. She is this way mainly to get a reaction.)

JULIE

(Flashes a peace sign.)

Hey, Wings. Peace, my main man. Is my dad here?

SERGEANT

I'm calling him right now and wait…yes, Captain…got a case of a stolen violin here. Can you come down for a minute?

(Pause.)

I think it's a long story.

(Hangs up.)

Stick around, maybe you can help out. And put out that cigarette. You know how that upsets your dad.

JULIE

(Stubs out the cigarette in a cup that's on the table and looks at the GYPSY, who is now sitting down right in one of the chairs.)

Chill out, fly boy. You gotta learn to stay frosty.

(Crosses to him.)

Okay if I knock back a Coca-Cola while waiting for the man?

SERGEANT

(Reaches into pocket.)

Need some change for the machine?

JULIE

No way, José. I stick a coat hanger up the slot and a chilly Coca-Cola's gonna drop right down into my hot little hand.

(She starts out right.)

SERGEANT

(Rises toward her.)

Don't let your dad see you do that. Don't let anybody see you do that.

(She's off stage. Louder.)

Some day we'll have to answer to the Coca-Cola Company, and then what?

(CAPTAIN enters.)

CAPTAIN

Stolen violin, what's the big deal?

SERGEANT

Ikey, it's complicated.

(Indicates the Gypsy.)

Ma'am.

CAPTAIN

(Extends his hand.)

Captain Jones, ma'am. And you are?

GYPSY

(She holds her hand to have it kissed. He tries to shake it.)

A gypsy.

CAPTAIN

Ah, right. I take it you have no ID, nothing…

SERGEANT

Ikey, she's a gypsy. They don't have ID or addresses. I told you this was going to be complicated.

CAPTAIN

Yes, I heard you.

(JULIE reenters.)

Your mother lets you go out dressed like that?

(He loves his daughter, but still has a hard time with her lifestyle. She loves him, too.)

JULIE
(She grabs his arms.)
This is nothing. She wears shorter skirts than I do. And, hey, you won't believe this, but she's dating a guy who owns a Harley. And he wears a helmet with swastikas on it. Far out.

CAPTAIN
So, your mother goes out nearly nude and she's dating a Nazi. Why am I not surprised?

JULIE
She said that's what you'd say. She says you are too buttoned down for her. She says the cleaners don't starch your shirts—they stuff them just for you.

CAPTAIN
And just what is that supposed to mean?

SERGEANT
Ikey, I think it means that you're too uptight.

CAPTAIN
I know what it means. Where'd your mother meet this biker?

JULIE
In a strip club. He's a member of the Bad Boys from Troy M.C.

SERGEANT
The M.C. means...
(The CAPTAIN gives him a look.)

JULIE
I asked him why he picked the Trojans, and he said because he didn't want to "get any vi-near-eal diseases." What an idiot.
(SERGEANT starts to laugh.)

CAPTAIN
(Gives him another look and takes out his money clip.)
Here's 20 bucks. Go out and have some fun with your friends tonight, but no drinking, no smoking, no drugs...and well, no anything else.
(He puts money clip back in his pocket.)
And have a good time.

JULIE
Jesus H. Chrysler, Maria Von Trapp couldn't have a good time with all those rules.

CAPTAIN
(Kisses her on the cheek.)
Watch your language, or did you pick that up from your mother and her biker boyfriend? Now, get out of here, and I do want you to have a good time.

JULIE
Go? But Wings said I might be of help, somehow.

CAPTAIN
No, this is just a routine theft. Go on home and change those clothes. Don't they wear uniforms at that school?

JULIE
That was at St. Catherine's a million years ago. Pop, I go to college now. Remember?

CAPTAIN
Then, college should have a dress code.

JULIE
Dad, you're so retro.
     (Now, she turns to go out and really looks at the GYPSY.)
Hey, sister, cool threads. Where did you get those earrings?

GYPSY
Vladivostok, from my grandmother.

JULIE
Hey, sister, heavy. You really look cool. Hey, is this your violin?

GYPSY
No, he was stolen from Ubermann.

CAPTAIN
Go on, Julie, I'll take care of this. It's just some scam probably. You know about gypsies.

GYPSY
Not scam. He's a Stradivarius.

JULIE
     (She looks into case.)
What? Dad, let me take a look.

CAPTAIN
Go on home. This is not your concern.

JULIE
     (Studies it without touching it.)
A possible Strad, and it's not my concern? I'm a music major at NYU, specializing in piano and...

SERGEANT
That'd be violin, Ikey.

CAPTAIN
Will you stay out of this!

JULIE
And you, my father, my own flesh and blood, don't value my highly educated opinion?

CAPTAIN
I should. I paid enough for it.

JULIE
And if you don't value it, I might as well bail out of school and become a member of the chorus in an off-off-Broadway show, a gypsy in the theatre, living in a one-room apartment with no hot water, smoking pot, drinking cheap wine and having sex with everybody who believes in free love.

SERGEANT
Are you trying to give your father a heart attack?

JULIE
No, I'm trying to get him to see that I'm an adult. People see me and mom together and think we're sisters.
CAPTAIN
That's not because you seem older. That's because your mother never grew up.
JULIE
No dad, it's because I have.
CAPTAIN
Your mother should be dating a banker, not a biker.
JULIE
Bankers are for squares. This biker dude's got the coolest bike ever made, man. The Blue Electroglide. Just like Robert Blake, the chilliest cop this side of the Nome PD. Nobody plays a cool cop like Robert Blake.
CAPTAIN
Robert Blake is nothing but a hoodlum. He's a star now, but he's going to be in big trouble someday. You wait and see.
JULIE
Robert Blake is the most righteous dude on the tube. He's more righteous than Bobby Hatfield and Bill Medley put together. And you can take that to the bank, Frank. Now, let's take a look at this violin. If it's a Strad, you better hold onto your hat.
    (She leans over the open case but doesn't touch the violin.)
GYPSY
Oh, it's a Stradivarius, but he must go home.
JULIE
Dad, if it's clean, give me your handkerchief.
    (He reaches for his back pocket, remembers that it's not clean, and gives her his breast pocket square. She takes it and lifts the violin out carefully by the neck and then with her bare hands lifts out the bow. This is done with the skill and respect of a concert violinist.)
The color is right. It needs cleaned up but this looks right so far. Ma'am, where did you get this?
GYPSY
My 'usban steal him from Ubermann.
SERGEANT
She's saying her husband stole it from some guy named Hubert Man, probably a pawnbroker.
JULIE
Are you saying this violin once belonged to Herr Ubermann, the concert violinist?
GYPSY
Yes. 'usban go backstage and steal him just before intermission.
JULIE
Hey. I know this story!

47

CAPTAIN
See, your education is going to pay off.

JULIE
Anybody who plays the fiddle at a square dance knows about Ubermann and his habit of always having two violins at every concert. Sometimes he switched off each night, sometimes he changed violins at intermission. One night he went back to his dressing room at intermission to change violins and the second was gone…and never found…so, no pawnbrokers involved.

GYPSY
My 'usban convinced stage door manager to let him in to listen from backstage, and he steal, but to play, not pawn. No repair or cleaning either since he knew anyone would recognize violin as Stradivarius.

JULIE
I believe her. This is the real thing!

CAPTAIN
How do we get in touch with this Ubermann?

JULIE
A séance…he's dead. But, he still has family here in New York. My violin teacher is a big fan. That's how I heard the story. He'll know how to get in touch with them, or he'll find out how.

CAPTAIN
Give me the number and I'll call your teacher. This is a police investigation, after all.

JULIE
Dad, there are no bad guys here. Let's just get this violin back to the rightful owners.

CAPTAIN
I agree, but I think your new friend here will want a reward.

JULIE
I think she deserves one, don't you?

CAPTAIN
That's up to the family. This is a stolen item, after all.

JULIE
(Taking out her memo book.)
She didn't steal it. She's returning it. Here's the number, and if you call right away, he'll probably still be at his office. And don't go peeking at the other numbers in the book. Just stick to the numbers for the Music Department.

CAPTAIN
I don't "peek" through other people's personal property.

JULIE
You do that all the time. It's part of your job. Just tell whoever answers that you want extension 77. If he's there, he'll pick up.

(The CAPTAIN uses the Sergeant's desk phone, while the Sergeant goes back to his paperwork. The Gypsy and JULIE cross right to the chairs. JULIE drinks her Coke.)

GYPSY
You say you want to be gypsy?

JULIE
That's right. A singer and dancer in the chorus. A gypsy traveling from show to show, never settling down, singing, dancing and always on the move. I want to get into a production of HAIR and take of my clothes at end of Act One… every night.

GYPSY
Gypsy dancer never take off her clothes until after the dance when her lover…

CAPTAIN
(He cuts in.)
I heard that, and she's too young for any of that.
(Into the phone.)
Give me extension 77.

JULIE
(Overlaps his line.)
You think I'm too young for everything.
(To GYPSY.)
When did you start dancing?

GYPSY
When I was 12.

JULIE
And when did you start taking lovers?

GYPSY
When I was 12.

JULIE
You were married when you were 12?

GYPSY
No, I had lovers when I was 12. I was married I was 13.

CAPTAIN
(Covers phone.)
Did you people know there are laws against that? Who do you think you are, Mrs. Jerry Lee Lewis?

GYPSY.
The gypsy lives by no law. The gypsy lives by the heart. The gypsy dance, play, laugh. The gypsy love. No law can govern that. The gypsy heart is free.

JULIE
Good golly, Miss Molly, you really are the coolest.

CAPTAIN
(Crosses to them.)
Now, Miss Gypsy, you can just cool your heels, then.
(To JULIE, as he gives back her address book.)
Your teacher is on his way over, and if this turns out to be the real McCoy…

GYPSY
He not McCoy…he Stradivarius.
CAPTAIN
That's what we're about to find out. If it's the real thing, then we'll get in touch with the family. He says he's sure they'll want to reward your friend here, and not press any charges. I'm going back to my office. Wings will call me when your prof gets here to make the identification. So, you two stay put for now.
JULIE
Nothing will get me to leave now. This is way too exciting. I mean, totally, like discovering King Tut, or something.
CAPTAIN
Remember, these things can be a blessing or a curse.
GYPSY
I know something about curse.
CAPTAIN
You mean, you know how to curse?
GYPSY
No, I mean, I know how to put a curse on someone.
CAPTAIN
Nobody believes in that stuff anymore.
GYPSY
People still subject to the power of the gypsy.
CAPTAIN
I'll believe in curses when I see one.
(He exits.)
GYPSY
There is curse for everything and everyone. And remember what your father said. Blessing or curse. What is curse for one is blessing for someone else.
JULIE
Like you can put a curse on my father to have an open mind. That would be a blessing for me.
GYPSY
Yes, but that would have to be powerful curse. Your father a stubborn man. Remind me of my father.
JULIE
Your father…I figure he was pretty open-minded, I mean, you had lovers at age 12. What was that like?
GYPSY
We were traveling through Europe and Hitler started to persecute gypsies as he persecute Jews, but SS officers like me…they like how I dance and to love. To save my father and mother, I dance. German officers fight over me, kill over me. They lust for gypsy woman who dance with bare leg…who glow and sweat in the firelight. Not like their pale, cold wives back in Berlin. The gypsy women make their blood boil, and they help me to bring my father and mother to America. I take 'usban and escape to freedom in the USA.

JULIE

You married a Nazi?

GYPSY

No, he just steal uniform and pretend. He really gypsy.

JULIE

And through all this, you somehow escaped to America?

GYPSY

Yes, but we have no work. We live in streets, dancing, stealing. We eat garbage from restaurants, we sleep in filthy blankets. We do things to shame us, but we survive. Then, my 'usban steal the violin. Then when he play and I dance, people throw money on the sidewalk and we get down on our hands and knees and smile and pick it up and go on. We know it is not us they throw money to but to violin. He sing to the audience of joy, and he speak of great sorrow. He warmed them from the cold, he feed their souls when they are starving. He save our lives. Suddenly, my 'usban, he play like no gypsy ever play, because no gypsy ever have a violin like that. All violins are carved from wood and held together with resin. But the Stradivarius, his rich red wood glow in the lamplight. The music make young girls swoon and grown men cry. He make beautiful ladies fall in love and kings envious. Soon, we become rich and leave New York forever.

JULIE

Far out. That's some story. But, why would you leave New York?

GYPSY

When young girls faint, we take their jewelry. When grown men cry, we steal their wallets. And when beautiful women fall in love, my husband take all of their gifts.

JULIE

So, the police were after you?

(GYPSY nods yes.)

Because you were stealing from everyone?

GYPSY

What do you want? We're gypsies.

JULIE

Where did you go?

GYPSY

Doughhio.

JULIE

Where?

GYPSY

Doughhio. Clevelan', Doughhio.

JULIE

You left New York and went to Cleveland, Ohio???

GYPSY

Yes, who would look for us there?

JULIE
I can't argue with that. And you stayed there until now?
GYPSY
Yes, my 'usban, he fall in love with bass ball, and all he is interested in is in the Indians of Clevelan'.
JULIE
Your husband watched baseball...
GYPSY
Yes, he watch it on TV, he listen on radio, he go to ballpark and say greatest food in America is frankfooter with mustard. Then, one day, they invite him to play Star-Spangled Banner.
JULIE
He played the national anthem on the violin?
GYPSY
Yes, he play at the series of all the world when the Indians of Clevelan' met the Giants of New York America. He play, and all the people remove their hats and put their hands over their hearts. And even the bass ball players have tears in their eyes. The violin, he sing to them love of their country, he sang of hope and living out dreams and having the will to go on. And to believe that something good can come from depression and war.
JULIE
Then what happened?
GYPSY
The Indians lose four straight games and go home in humiliation. My 'usban lose all his money betting and that's why he became a bigamist marrying rich old women. Then, when he go to jail, I bring violin here to go home.
JULIE
That is one amazing story.
GYPSY
What is your name?
JULIE
Well, my mom named me Honeysuckle...she's a free thinker...Honeysuckle Jones.
GYPSY
I like that. It suits you.
JULIE
But, my dad insisted I have the middle name Juliet, so most people call me Julie. He's real conservative.
GYPSY
I saw. He does seem starched and ironed all over.
JULIE
Yes, he does, but he is a wonderful father. Just the wrong man for my mom to marry.
GYPSY
This school you attend. Is very expensive?

JULIE

Yes, very expensive.

GYPSY

Your father, he pay for all this?

JULIE

I got some scholarships, but he pays the rest. And I do take private violin lessons. That's expensive, too.

GYPSY

Then this money from the reward would be of help to you at the school?

JULIE

Yes, but I...

GYPSY

(She starts out.)

Then I give the money to you.

[EXCERPT FROM STAGE PLAY]

TELEVISION/MOVIE SCRIPT WINNER

CUT

Maureen Olund
Houston, TX

FADE IN: INT. HOUSE - ELIZABETH'S BEDROOM – SUNSET

Sun rays beam through the window into a warmly lit room. ELIZABETH, 13, lies like a corpse atop her twin-sized bed. She is engulfed in an oversized sweatshirt and baggy sweatpants. Elizabeth stares with fixed eyes at her ceiling.

On Elizabeth's stomach lies a stuffed teddy bear face-down. Elizabeth caresses the bear. Elizabeth rubs him up and down her pelvis. Her breath quickens. Moans are heard in her silent exhales. Her face is stoic.

MOTHER, 43 going on 24, is heard howling in the distance.

                    MOTHER (OFF-SCREEN)
Elizabeth!

Elizabeth ignores Mother's yells. She rubs the teddy bear up and down, up and down.

                    MOTHER (O.S.) (CONT'D)
Elizabeth! Elizabeth!

MATCH CUT TO: INT. OFFICE BUILDING - COMPANY CHRISTMAS PARTY - AFTERNOON (FLASHBACK)

Elizabeth, 8, fidgets amongst mingling men and women. A white-lit Christmas tree glistens and a colorful banner reads "Happy Holidays". A woman pounds "Let It Snow" on the piano.

FATHER, 40, glides toward Elizabeth from across the room. He is dressed in a fine black suit. Women sneak glances at him as he passes by.

                    FATHER
Elizabeth! Elizabeth!

Elizabeth holds a glass of eggnog and tugs at her puffy green-and-silver dress. She smiles.

SLAM CUT TO: ELIZABETH'S BEDROOM (PRESENT)

Elizabeth grinds the teddy bear back and forth. Her sweatshirt lifts on her stomach to reveal both fresh and scabbed-over cuts on her abdomen.

SLAM CUT TO: COMPANY CHRISTMAS PARTY (FLASHBACK)

Father sweeps Elizabeth up in his arms. She giggles. He hugs her tight and they dance to the music. Elizabeth tugs at her dress to keep it from riding up. Mother, 38, eyes the two dancing from across the room.

SLAM CUT TO: ELIZABETH'S BEDROOM (PRESENT)

Elizabeth yanks her sweatshirt back down over her abdomen. She focuses again on stroking the bear up and down, even harder.

MOTHER (O.S.)
Help your brother! Where are you?

Elizabeth hums to drown out Mother's yelling.

CUT TO: COMPANY CHRISTMAS PARTY (FLASHBACK)

Elizabeth smiles at Father as they dance. Her dress rides up to reveal her tights and white underwear. Father looks down. Elizabeth covers her thighs with her hands. Father then looks away.

CUT TO: ELIZABETH'S BEDROOM (PRESENT)

Elizabeth lies still as the teddy bear rests on her hips. Her breath is back to a normal pace.

MOTHER (O.S.)
ELIZABETH! Help your brother!

CUT TO: COMPANY CHRISTMAS PARTY (FLASHBACK)

Father sets her down immediately. Elizabeth tugs on her dress. The two are not laughing anymore. Father grabs a glass of wine from the table and walks over to Mother standing across the room. Mother looks away from Father when he comes near her.

CUT TO: ELIZABETH'S BEDROOM (PRESENT)

Elizabeth hugs the teddy bear to her chest. She stands up and sets the teddy bear on the pillow.

INT. HOUSE - HALLWAY

A dim hallway. Stains tattoo the carpet. The walls are bare. Blue iridescent light flickers from the room at the end of the hallway. A door opens. Elizabeth ambles out of her bedroom. She tugs at her sweatshirt and saunters down the hallway toward the

LIVING ROOM

Papers clutter the dingy room. Foil has been molded on top of the television into a make-shift antenna. Mother is sprawled out on the couch. She sips a beer in one hand and holds the remote control in the other. Many more empty cans are dispersed over the table. Mother glances up at Elizabeth, then turns back to the television.

                    MOTHER
Where were you? He's in the kitchen.

Elizabeth enters the KITCHEN. It is separated by an archway from the living room. The patterned tiles on the floor are washed-out and crud is wedged in their crevices. The appliances are outdated and the only natural light comes from a small window above the sink.

HENRY, 22, the mentally challenged brother, gawks at the oven. He wears oven mitts on both hands. His hair is in a mad array. He begins to chant at the oven.

                    HENRY
Hum, deee-leee, hum...

Elizabeth peers from the archway. She whispers.

                    ELIZABETH
Henry...what are you doing?

                    HENRY
AHH!

Henry stares at Elizabeth for a good while, then giggles and barges toward her.

>   HENRY (CONT'D)
> Hug! E!

Elizabeth dodges Henry and moves toward the oven.

>   ELIZABETH
> No, Henry. Cut it out.

>   HENRY
> Your help!

Elizabeth sees that the oven is turned off.

>   ELIZABETH
> Yeah, you need something.

Elizabeth fiddles with a knob on the stove.

>   ELIZABETH (CONT'D)
> What were you trying to do?

>   HENRY
> Cook!

>   ELIZABETH
> You have to turn it on first.

BEEPS come from the pre-heating timer.

>   HENRY
> Dance! Music!

Henry dances to the BEEPING.

>   ELIZABETH
> Henry, you have to turn it on. Always. You can't just yell at it.

Elizabeth takes hold of the oven mitts on Henry's hands.

>   ELIZABETH (CONT'D)
> Here. Give me those.

>   HENRY
> AHH! My claws!

Elizabeth rips them off his hands.

> ELIZABETH
> You look silly Henry.

Henry jogs into the LIVING ROOM. Henry scrambles across the couch.

> MOTHER
> Henry, calm down.

Henry plops onto the floor in the corner. His legs sprawl out into a V-shape. Before him lie scattered sheets of paper and colored markers.

> HENRY
> E helped me!

> MOTHER
> Shhh. Go in there if you're gonna talk.

Mother turns up the volume on the television until Henry beats at his ears.

> HENRY
> AHH! It hurts!

Mother turns the volume back down.

> MOTHER
> Then be quiet.

Elizabeth enters.

> ELIZABETH
> Mom, what do I make Henry for dinner?

> MOTHER
> Whatever we got.

> ELIZABETH
> Mom, we don't have anything.

> MOTHER
> Yes we do. I just bought stuff the other day.

> ELIZABETH
> When?

                            MOTHER
          Damnit Elizabeth. Enough. We have food. We ain't starvin.

Elizabeth exits into the KITCHEN.

Elizabeth opens the refrigerator door, peers inside, then slams it shut. She opens the freezer, letting some rancid odor pour out, causing her to cover her mouth and nose with one hand. She grabs a bag of frozen chicken tenders and slams the door shut.

INT. LIVING ROOM

TOM, 47, Mother's boyfriend, staggers through the front door. He is a burly man with a snake-skin belt that hides beneath his protruding belly.

                            TOM
          Ho! Ho! Ho!

Tom grabs his belly and shakes it up and down.

                        TOM (CONT'D)
          Big papa's gotta treat.

Tom pulls out a clear bag from his pocket. Inside appear tiny dried grass blades.

                    TOM (TO MOTHER) (CONT'D)
          Damn, you look good lyin' down.

                            HENRY
          Hi Tom!

                            TOM
          Yo Henry!

Henry springs up to give Tom a hug. They take hold of one another. Tom hoists Henry up until his feet lift off the ground.

                            HENRY
          Ugh! Ugh!

Tom squeezes Henry until he gasps for air. Henry struggles to touch the floor with his feet.

                          TOM
            Who da man! You da man? I da man?

                         MOTHER
            Tom! Put him down. He ain't as strong as you.

                          HENRY
            Ugh! Ugh!

Tom releases Henry, who falls to the floor. Tom struts to the couch and sits on Mother's stomach. Henry crawls back to his corner while moaning from pain.

                         MOTHER
            Baby get off!
                          TOM
            Wah? I thought you liked to be sat on.

Henry forgets he was in pain.

                          HENRY
            Spat on. Ha, ha.

Mother slaps the side of Tom.

                         MOTHER
            Whatever...shut up.

(BACK TO KITCHEN)

Elizabeth hunches over the sink. She struggles to tear open the frozen bag. She drops the bag and ventures to a drawer, extracting a long pair of scissors. Elizabeth stands by the sink and cuts at the bag. She yells to Henry.

                        ELIZABETH
            Henry, what else do you want to eat?

(BACK TO LIVING ROOM)

                          HENRY
            Apples and peanubutta! Yay!

Tom strikes a match on the couch.

(BACK TO KITCHEN)

Elizabeth spreads the chicken tenders onto a baking sheet.

>   ELIZABETH
> With chicken? Peanut butter? Are you sure?

Coughs are heard from Tom.

>   ELIZABETH (CONT'D)
> Tom, uh can you smoke that outside?

>   TOM (O.S.)
> Ah, wassup Lizzy?

>   ELIZABETH
> Can you smoke outside?

(BACK TO LIVING ROOM)

Mother laughs into the pillow of the couch. Tom inhales his smoke.

>   TOM
> Ah, well, your mom doesn't...

(BACK TO KITCHEN)

Elizabeth opens the window above the sink.

>   TOM (O.S.)
> Sorry Lizzy!

Elizabeth throws the baking sheet into the oven and slams the door shut. Elizabeth stands at the sink. The setting sun's rays pound onto her face. She shuts her eyes.

SLAM CUT TO: EXT. SIDEWALK - AFTERNOON (FLASHBACK)

The setting sun blinds a fumbling Elizabeth, 12, and the only thing guiding her is the hand of Mother. Henry holds Mother's other hand. The three of them rush down a street.

>   ELIZABETH
> Mom, but why?

They hustle across an intersection as the light turns green and cars begin to approach them.

                    ELIZABETH (CONT'D)
            Henry could have done this.

                         MOTHER
            I already told you Elizabeth!

A passing car honks at them. Mother throws the driver her middle-finger.

                    MOTHER (CONT'D)
            FUCK YOU!

(BEAT)

            Will you two hurry up. Now?

                        ELIZABETH
            He could have gone with you. I was in school.

                         MOTHER
            ENOUGH! No he couldn't.

                        ELIZABETH
            You're just going to Social Services, right? Why did you need both
            of us? You only need one of us with you. All he had to do was stand
            there.

                         MOTHER
            JESUS! Elizabeth, you just don't stop do you? I can't get our check
            unless one of you claims I'm still in charge of you. FUCK. He
            couldn't claim a damn thing.

                        ELIZABETH
            He's retarded, not deaf.

Henry trips on the sidewalk and stumbles forward.

                         MOTHER
            DAMNIT. Get up Henry.
SLAM CUT TO: KITCHEN (PRESENT)

Elizabeth extracts a knife from a drawer. She quarters an apple.

                        HENRY (O.S.)
            E! Slice the apples flat! Like pannycakes!

GIGGLES are heard from Mother and Tom on the couch. Elizabeth begins to slice the apple into slivers. She cuts once, twice, when the knife slips and slices her thumb. Blood trickles onto the counter.

> ELIZABETH
> Fuck.

Elizabeth wraps her thumb in the sleeve of her sweatshirt. She moves to the archway.

LIVING ROOM

Tom is rolling another joint.

> ELIZABETH
> Tom, are you going out again?

Blood seeps into the fabric of Elizabeth's sleeve.

> TOM
> Why you ask?

> ELIZABETH
> We don't have any peanut butter.

> HENRY
> No peanut butta?

> ELIZABETH
> It's okay Henry.

> MOTHER
> I just bought some.

> ELIZABETH
> No. We don't have any peanut butter. Tom can you get some if you go out again?

> TOM (TO MOTHER)
> More beer?

Mother stares at the television. She does not answer.

> HENRY
> What? No peanut butta?

> TOM (TO ELIZABETH)
> Yeah, I'm gettin' another twelve-pack. I'll grab some of that too.

> ELIZABETH
> Thank you.

> HENRY
> BUT THE PEANUT BUTTA?

> TOM
> Shit man, I'm gettin' some.

> ELIZABETH
> Henry, you'll get your peanut butter.

Henry is relieved and begins to color again. Elizabeth turns and walks back into the KITCHEN. Elizabeth stands at the sink. Tom enters. He opens the refrigerator.

> TOM
> And what do I get in return?

Elizabeth is silent. Tom pulls out two beers chuckling to himself. He exits.

> TOM (O.S.) (CONT'D)
> Peace! I'm out.

Elizabeth runs water over her thumb and the front DOOR SLAM is heard. Mother strolls into the kitchen. She opens the refrigerator and pulls out a beer.

> MOTHER
> You know, you aren't in charge here.

> ELIZABETH
> I know.

> MOTHER
> Yeah, don't act like it.

> ELIZABETH
> Huh?

Mother slams the refrigerator door shut.

> MOTHER
> I said don't act like it.

> ELIZABETH
> I never said I was in charge.

> MOTHER
> Your little sass ain't flyin' with me.

> ELIZABETH
> I wasn't. I'm not in charge. Okay?

> MOTHER
> DAMNIT Elizabeth. I can't deal with it anymore. You think you're so tough.

> ELIZABETH
> No I don't.

> MOTHER
> Ever since he left you think you're so goddamn tough.

> ELIZABETH
> WHO?

> MOTHER
> Shut up.

Mother walks out of the kitchen.

> ELIZABETH
> WHO? Nobody left!

(PAUSE)

> ELIZABETH (CONT.)
> Say his name.

Elizabeth sneaks out of the kitchen. She retreats to ELIZABETH'S BEDROOM. Elizabeth slams her door shut. She walks in full circles around her room cursing herself. Elizabeth steps over to her bed, snags the teddy bear, and in the pocket of its ear she extracts a blade. She lies on her bed.

Elizabeth pulls up her sweatshirt and cuts a deep gash onto her right hip.

The blood oozes. She rushes over to her closet. Elizabeth pulls out a balled-up T-shirt stained with dried blood. She covers the cut with the T-shirt. Elizabeth lies back down on her bed.

LIVING ROOM – NIGHT

Tom enters the front door. He carries two twenty-four-packs of beer.

>TOM
>FUCK!

Henry, coloring on the floor, covers his ears in shock. Mother sits up on the couch.

>MOTHER
>What?

Tom stands in the open doorway.

>TOM
>I knew it. I knew it. I remember standin' in the store…sayin' 'don't forget the peanut butter, don't forget the peanut butter'…And what do I do?

(BEAT)

>FUCK. I forgot it!

Mother stares at Tom.

>MOTHER
>You're an idiot.

>HENRY
>No peanut butta?

>TOM
>I know! I'm getting fuckin' old. Shit man. I'm supposed to remember I'm gonna forget things but I can't even fuckin' remember that!

>MOTHER
>Go put those in the fridge.

Tom tramples into the kitchen.

                              TOM
         Shit...fuck...

Henry peers around the room with his hands in ready-mode to cover his
ears again.

                              HENRY
         Potty potty mouth.

Tom re-enters the living room. Tom waddles down the HALLWAY.
He cups his rear side with his hands. He tilts his head back while he strains
to hold his bowel movement.

                              TOM
         Ooh. Aah. Ooh. Eeh.

LIVING ROOM

Mother laughs to herself as she flips through the channels on the television.

                              MOTHER
         He's better than anythin' on this damn TV.

Tom is heard stomping down the hallway.

                              TOM (O.S.)
         Just let me take a crap in peace, will you!

                              MOTHER
         Oh god.

                              HENRY
         Crap. Ha, ha. Crap...

BATHROOM

Yellowish tiles contrast the washed-out blue wallpaper. Tom hovers on the
toilet.

                              TOM
         I ain't no weather man, but this forecast's havin' rainstorms...

Tom chuckles to himself.

(BACK TO LIVING ROOM)

Henry holds up a drawing towards Mother. She takes hold of it and squints.

                      MOTHER
What is it?

                      HENRY
It's you, silly! In a dress, on a rainbow.

                      TOM (O.S.)
...Nah. It's gonna blow like a volcano!

Mother shakes her head at Tom. She peers at the picture.

                      MOTHER
Well, it don't look like me. But...thanks. I'll keep it.

(BACK TO BATHROOM)

Tom is red in the face. He twines toilet paper around his hand and wipes. He brings the wad up an inch away from his face. Tom sniffs.

                      TOM
Ah, shit. Honey!

Mother is heard laughing.

                      TOM (CONT'D)
This shit don't look right!

(BACK TO LIVING ROOM)

Mother sips at her beer.

                      MOTHER
I smell you from here! Damn.

                      HENRY
Smells like poo poo!

Henry hunches over a marker. He sniffs.

                      MOTHER
Henry! Don't do that. You gonna kill the only brain cells you got.

                      HENRY
Purple, pupil, purple.

(BACK TO BATHROOM)

Tom moseys out of the bathroom zipping up his pants and moseys into the HALLWAY. His belt hangs undone. He knocks on Elizabeth's closed door.

ELIZABETH (O.S.)
Yeah?

TOM
Don't mind the scent. My brand can be a little strong. Whew!

Tom snickers. He continues down the HALLWAY. He enters the LIVING ROOM. Mother and Henry look up.

TOM
That shit ain't right!

ELIZABETH'S BEDROOM

Elizabeth lies on her bed reading a book. She is still pressing the T-shirt against her hip.

INT. SCHOOL BUS - MORNING

Elizabeth steps onto the school bus. A handful of boys and girls eye her as she surveys for a place to sit. They avoid her glances when she looks for the empty spots next to them. Elizabeth ambles to an empty row and sits.

Behind Elizabeth sit two pretty girls, one BLONDE and one BRUNETTE. They are dressed alike in pink and purple jumpsuits.

BRUNETTE (TO BLONDE)
Oh my god! So John was sitting towards the front of class yesterday when I read my poem.

Elizabeth stares out the window as the streets pass by.

BRUNETTE (CONT'D)
I think I saw his eyes tearing up. I swear! I was like 'John, are you crying?' And he was like 'No' and I was like 'Oh my god...!' It was so sweet!

The Blonde takes a dainty bite of her apple.

                    BLONDE
I was so nervous when I had to read mine.

                    BRUNETTE
Aw! But it was so good!

They look at each other and giggle. Elizabeth knocks the back of her head on the seat.

                    BLONDE (TO ELIZABETH)
Ummmmm, could you please stop that?

                    ELIZABETH
Yeah, okay.

Elizabeth stops. She slouches her body low so her head cannot be seen from behind.

                    BRUNETTE
Yeah, no kidding. So annoying. ANYWAYS...

The bus pulls in front of EXT. SCHOOL BUILDING – MORNING
A sign reads BIRKES JUNIOR HIGH. An American flag sways in the wind. A hand-made poster above the main entrance reads 'Stomp the Tigers!' Kids file out of the bus and through the double doors of the school.

The Brunette and Blonde step off simultaneously.

                    BRUNETTE (TO BLONDE)
Wow, your barrette looks like a cockroach.

                    BLONDE
Shut up!

                    BRUNETTE
No! It's cute! Totally cute!

                    BLONDE
Shut up!

They giggle. Elizabeth steps off and treks alone into the school building.

INT. - CLASSROOM

Incoming students organize into desks. The TEACHER, late 40s, leans against his desk in the front of the room. His shoulder-length hair parts down the center and his t-shirt reads 'Drink More Tea.' Elizabeth sits toward the rear of the classroom.

> **TEACHER**
> Hey. Alright, coffee break over! Did everyone finish their exponential equations from last night?

A BOY towards the front raises his hand.

> **BOY**
> YA. I didn't understand the homework. My dad and I spent freakin' three hours doing it. I missed "Speed Racer"...AGAIN!

Laughter from the classroom.

> **TEACHER**
> Funny, funny. Okay, well, try watching less mindless television first of all and practice the lessons I give you. There's a reason I stand up here everyday while you all moan and groan. I like attention but this isn't what I call my big break at a one-man show.

(BEAT)

> What didn't you get?

> **BOY**
> Everything.

> **TEACHER**
> Smart ass.

Laughter throughout the class. The Teacher goes into explaining logarithms. Elizabeth fixates on a boy sitting in front of her.

(DREAM)

The boy turns around and mouths the words "I love you." He then stands on his desk chair and clamors like an ape.
(END OF DREAM)

Elizabeth snickers to herself.

> **TEACHER**
> Elizabeth? Did you hear me? Elizabeth? What did you get for

number two?

Elizabeth stares at the Teacher. She does not reply. The Teacher waits.
She gives him nothing. Elizabeth chuckles. The class is silent and staring.
She then shrieks with laughter.

                    TEACHER (CONT'D)
          I think you should go to the bathroom Elizabeth. Come back when
          you are composed.

Elizabeth steps out into the SCHOOL HALLWAY. She stifles more
laughing. Murmurs are heard from inside the classroom.

                    TEACHER (O.S.)
     Jack! Number two!

Elizabeth walks down the hallway and enters the GIRL'S BATHROOM.
A young girl washes her hands at one of the many sinks against the wall.
Elizabeth strides to the stall at the far end. She shuts the door and sits
on the toilet. Elizabeth begins to pee. The young girl is heard leaving the
bathroom.

Elizabeth still holds her pencil in her hand. She rubs the pointed lead.
She draws a line on her exposed thigh with the pencil, then retraces
the line again. An incision is made on her leg. Elizabeth falls into a stupor.

EXT. BEACH - DAY (DREAM)

The dream is fragmented, flashing to black after every few seconds.
The sun beams onto the glistening sea. Waves splash onto the white sand.
The beach is completely empty except for two palm trees that suspend a
woven hammock holding Father and herself. Elizabeth lies her head on his
bare chest as he strokes her hair.

                    FATHER
     Sleep.

Elizabeth gazes out at the sea. Father brushes the hair out of her face.
Elizabeth looks out at the sea, hiding her tears from her Father. Father sees
her tears and looks away.

A flood of black.
(END OF DREAM)

INT. GIRL'S BATHROOM

A GIRL is staring at Elizabeth with the stall door wide open. Elizabeth has her eyes closed but tears run down her face.

                        GIRL
            What the fuck is wrong with you?

Elizabeth jolts. She glances up at the Girl. The Girl pulls out her cell phone from her back pocket.

                    GIRL (CONT'D)
            Hon, you need some fucking help.

Elizabeth pulls up her pants.

                    GIRL (CONT'D)
            You're bleeding...

She pushes the Girl out of the way and sprints into the HALLWAY. The Girl peeks out from the bathroom.

                        GIRL
            What the hell?

Elizabeth ducks into the CLASSROOM. The Teacher sits at his desk reading "Wake Up You Zombies" while the class works on their lessons. Elizabeth runs to her desk and grabs her backpack.

                      TEACHER
            Back to join us?

Elizabeth pants, trying to catch her breath. She begins to open her mouth. The class stares. The teacher stares. She darts out of the classroom.

                  TEACHER (CONT'D)
            Wait! Elizabeth!

HALLWAY

The Teacher steps into the hallway and watches Elizabeth burst through the double doors.

INT. ELIZABETH'S HOUSE - KITCHEN - EVENING

Elizabeth sits at the table staring at the floor. Mother strolls in. She rubs her head and looks away from Elizabeth.

MOTHER
Elizabeth. Can you worry about dinner tonight? I'm not feeling good.

ELIZABETH
Yeah.

MOTHER
Yeah, okay.

Mother exits the kitchen. She walks through the LIVING ROOM. Mother steps on papers scattered on the floor, including the drawing from Henry. She retreats to her bedroom.

A DOOR SLAM is heard off-screen.

Elizabeth enters. Henry sits on the couch. He covers his mouth in shock. A MALE VOICE explains the process of making American hot dogs on the television.

MALE VOICE (V.O.)
...squeezed into casing, cooked, then removed and packaged for wholesale. Americans consume over 16 billion hot dogs annually...

Elizabeth sits down next to him on the couch. Henry does not notice her.

ELIZABETH
Hey Henry. What are you watching?

Henry turns his head slowly to Elizabeth with his hands still over his gaped mouth and wide eyes.

ELIZABETH (CONT'D)
Stop that Henry.

Henry grabs Elizabeth before she can escape his hold. He squeezes her.

ELIZABETH (CONT'D)
Henry! Get OFF!

Elizabeth struggles to push him away.

ELIZABETH (CONT'D)
Okay, okay. I can't breath Henry.

Henry lets go.

> HENRY
> E! I'm so scared! Hotdogs! E, they scare me!

> ELIZABETH
> That's crazy. They can't be scary. Oscar Meyer is anything but scary.

> MALE VOICE (V.O.)
> ...Frankfurters, franks, red hots, wieners...

Henry is transfixed on the television again. Elizabeth picks up a piece of paper from off the coffee table. She studies it then sets it on her lap and turns to look at Henry.

> ELIZABETH
> Henry, why did you draw this?

The drawing is of a beach.

> MALE VOICE (V.O.)
> The cellulose casings are cut away leaving only the bare hot dogs... from the peeler they are transported to packaging.

> HENRY
> That's where you will live E!

(BEAT)

> Silly.

Elizabeth stares at Henry. Henry stares at the television.

> ELIZABETH
> Why do you think I'll live there?

> MALE VOICE (V.O.)
> Fats in the meat give the dog its characteristic flavor. Sometimes variety meats are used like liver however...

> HENRY
> E! It's pink! Why is it PINK?

Elizabeth picks up the paper again. Her eyes are glued on the drawing.

ELIZABETH
Why am I going to live here?

HENRY
Silly, you told dad so! That's where you will live. You said it like a million-gazillion times!

MALE VOICE (V.O.)
New varieties are being introduced...such as the cheese-containing hot dog. A product which is injected with a cheese sauce during manufacture...

HENRY
E! Are you scared? I'm scared!

Elizabeth stares at the picture, then back up at Henry.

ELIZABETH
Henry, what do you want to eat?

HENRY
Never, hot dogs, never again!

LAUGHS are heard from Mother's bedroom.

TOM (O.S.)
Like a lion! Tame this lion! ROAR.

Elizabeth sets the drawing on the table and stands up.

ELIZABETH
I can't listen to this.

She enters the kitchen.

ELIZABETH (O.S.) (CONT'D)
Wanna order some pizza?

HENRY
Yay! Pisa! Pisa!

INT. BATHROOM - NIGHT

Elizabeth draws herself a bath. Steam rises from the tub. She releases her hair from her low-ponytail. She looks at herself in the mirror. She grabs her bare chest with both hands. She squeezes her breasts. She stares at her figure in the mirror.

Elizabeth steps into the bathtub. She submerges her body slowly into the water. Closing both eyes she feels for the razor on the ledge. With the razor, she pricks her thumb. She pricks her wrist. Blood dissolves into the water.

KNOCKING is heard from the door.

                    HENRY
E? E? I have to use the potty.

                    ELIZABETH
Henry. Can't you just go, um, outside?

                    HENRY
OUTSIDE? Like puppies do?

                    ELIZABETH
I am in the bath.

                    HENRY
I'm scared.

                    ELIZABETH
It's okay. Just go in the back of the house.

                    HENRY
Like a dog?

Elizabeth closes her eyes. STUMBLES are heard outside the bathroom door. Tom jiggles the handle.

                    TOM
Hello? Who's in there?

                    ELIZABETH
Um, yeah. It's me.

                    TOM
Shit, I gotta piss Lizzy.

Tom bangs on the door.

                    TOM (CONT'D)
Just let me in. PLEASE.

(BEAT)

    I promise I won't look too much.

Tom shuffles back into the bedroom.

Elizabeth stands up in the bathtub. She steps out onto the bathroom tile, standing in a puddle of water. She wraps herself in a towel and steps into the HALLWAY.

Mother rushes out of her bedroom.

          MOTHER
    No! No you asshole. DON'T touch me!

Tom exits the bedroom and grabs a hold of her arm.

          TOM
    Stop that! I was just fuckin' around!

Mother yanks away from Tom's grasp.

          MOTHER
    NO! Get the fuck away from me! Out, just get the fuck out you fuck!

Tom pouts his lips.

          TOM
    Baby! Don't be like that...

Elizabeth looks at her Mother. Mother charges toward Elizabeth. Mother walks straight up to her and slaps Elizabeth across the face.

          MOTHER
    You...

Mother points accusingly at her with disgust.

          MOTHER (CONT'D)
    You...you bitch. You think you're so cute and clever, huh?

Elizabeth touches her cheek.

                   ELIZABETH
What?

                      TOM
Baby! Cut that out. She didn't do anything.

                    MOTHER
No. No. She's done everything. This bitch is the reason everything is wrong.

(BEAT)

You...you thought you were so clever...so smart? You think I didn't know? Thought he wanted you more than me? MORE THAN ME?

(BEAT)

Well your father isn't here anymore, is he? Look who's all alone now.

Tom stands frozen in the bedroom doorway. Mother and Elizabeth stare at one another. Elizabeth's body shakes from rage.

                      TOM
Stop this. You gotta stop this.

Mother turns toward Tom.

                    MOTHER
No. You shut the fuck up! You want her too?

                      TOM
All I said was sure. You asked me. I didn't bring it up. Sure if she were older. If I weren't with you.

Mother faces Elizabeth.

                    MOTHER
I knew you wanted her. You can have the little slut. Just hope you don't mind sloppy seconds.

Mother storms back into her bedroom pushing Tom out of the way and slamming the door behind her. Elizabeth's body trembles.

> **TOM**
> Lizzy...I...

> **ELIZABETH**
> No....please.

Elizabeth retreats to her bedroom shutting the door quietly behind her.

INT. ELIZABETH'S BEDROOM - DAWN

Elizabeth looks around. She picks up a tiny, pink pig figurine off her desk. She wraps it in a T-shirt and tucks it away in her duffel bag. One by one she packs up her belongings. Elizabeth tip-toes over to the mirror. She studies her reflection.

Elizabeth picks up the teddy bear and places it on the top of her bag. She zips everything up and lulls the bag into the HALLWAY. Elizabeth opens the door to Henry's bedroom. She watches him sleep from the doorway. She moves over to his bed.

> **ELIZABETH**
> I'm sorry. I can't. I just can't.

She pets his hair. Henry stirs. He opens his eyes.

> **ELIZABETH (CONT'D)**
> Henry, go back to sleep. I didn't mean to wake you...

> **HENRY**
> E? Where are you going?

> **ELIZABETH**
> I'm...I am leaving.

> **HENRY**
> I'm sleepy E.

> **ELIZABETH**
> I'm not leaving you...but I have to leave.

Elizabeth cries.

> **HENRY**
> Love you E.

                    ELIZABETH
I love you too Henry. I will always love you. I just...

                    HENRY
Are you leaving E?

                    ELIZABETH
Yes Henry.

Elizabeth bends down. She hugs him.

                    ELIZABETH (CONT'D)
I will come back Henry, for you.

                    HENRY
Like daddy?

                    ELIZABETH
Um, no. I will be back. I promise.

Elizabeth unzips her bag and pulls out the Teddy Bear. She gives it to Henry.

                    HENRY
Teddy!

                    ELIZABETH
Keep it.

                    HENRY
But you love Teddy.

                    ELIZABETH
Take care of him until I come back.

Elizabeth stands up. She walks to the door. She fights back tears.

                    ELIZABETH (CONT'D)
Go back to sleep. I love you.

Elizabeth closes the door. She tiptoes down the HALLWAY into the LIVING ROOM. Henry's drawings are dispersed over the floor. Beer cans cover the table. Tom's belt hangs over the arm of the couch. Elizabeth walks over to the table and picks up the drawing of the beach.

                              ELIZABETH
                    Henry...

Elizabeth folds the paper many times into a tiny square. She stuffs it into her pocket.

EXT. FRONT YARD - SUNRISE

The sun casts an orange glow onto the neighborhood. Elizabeth squints her eyes. She lifts her hand to shield the sun's rays. Cuts are shown on her wrist.

(DREAM)

The row of houses morphs into crashing waves. The light pole on the street transforms into a palm tree.
(END OF DREAM)

Elizabeth picks up her duffel bag and walks down to the sidewalk from her yard. From there, she treads down the street to the corner bus stop. Minutes pass. A bus crawls into view. It stops in front of Elizabeth. She squints from the rising sun rays. Her face cannot be seen from the sun's glare.

                              FADE OUT.

CHILDREN'S/YOUNG ADULT FICTION WINNERS

1. Amy J. Finnegan
   Highland UT
2. Susanna Hill
   Poughquag NY
3. Amy Finnegan
   Highland UT
4. Kathleen E. Fearing
   Clinton TN
5. Heather Meloche
   Rochester Hills MI
6. Robert West
   Moses Lake WA
7. Jean Reagan
   Salt Lake City UT
8. Jamie Michalak
   Barrington RI
9. Amy Dominy
   Phoenix AZ
10. Rita M. Tubbs
    Vanderbilt MI
11. Lori Anastasia
    North Attleboro MA
12. Lauren Carson
    East Falmouth MA
13. Toni Babcock
    South Saint Paul MN
14. Pepper Basham
    Elizabethton TN
15. Angela Cerrito
    Sedro Woolley WA
16. Terilee Wunderman
    Miami FL
17. Patti Kurtz
    Minot ND
18. Carol Tarlow
    Kula HI
19. Gwen P Johnson
    Tallahassee FL
20. Jodi Stewart
    Haslet TX
21. Brenda Nelson-Davis
    Brookfield WI
22. Norma Lewis
    Byron Center MI
23. Tammy Wright
    Neligh NE
24. Nancy Takemori
    Tampa FL
25. Tom Clark
    Loveland OH
26. Gary Hill
    Bakersfield CA
27. Julie Riuinus
    Clayton MO
28. Stephanie Armiger
    Twin Falls ID
29. Amy Dominy
    Phoenix AZ
30. Sarah Welle
    Oswego KS
31. Sarah Welle
    Oswego KS
32. Sheila Romano
    Elk Grove CA
33. Lauren King
    Wichita KS
34. Syrl Kazlo
    Fort Ann NY

35. Marie Mitchell
    Richmond KY
36. Cindy Antene
    Brookfield IL
37. Patricia Corcoran
    New Milford CT
38. Jamie Michalak
    Barrington RI
39. Dana Konop
    Canton GA
40. Katie Beatty
    Fruitland NM
41. Katia Raina
    Manahawkin NJ
42. Marie Etzler
    Davie FL
43. Alexandra Parsons
    New York NY
44. Heather Kolich
    Cumming GA
45. Marie Mitchell
    Richmond KY
46. Ken Kilback
    Burnaby BC Canada
47. Janelle Bitikofer
    Raleigh NC
48. Michele Peterson
    Fresno CA
49. Stacey Velazquez
    Edgewood NM
50. Doris Cavallin
    Orleans ON Canada
51. Ken Kilback
    Burnaby BC Canada
52. Sarah Tregay
    Eagle ID
53. Katie Beatty
    Fruitland NM
54. Renee LeVerrier
    Newburyport MA
55. Renee LeVerrier
    Newburyport MA
56. Janet Park
    Seattle WA
57. Elizabeth Ashley Walker
    Charlotte NC
58. David Zuppke
    Lebanon NH
59. Amy Dominy
    Phoenix AZ
60. Laurie Alloway
    San Diego CA
61. Eleanor Langford
    Algood TN
62. Ruth Maxwell
    Seattle WA
63. Jennifer Bohnhoff
    Albuquerque NM
64. Giselle Rondon
    Trincity Trinidad and Tobago
65. Kathleen St. Claire
    Menlo Park CA
66. Mary Lash
    Piedmont SC
67. Jan O'Connor
    North Hollywood CA

68. Tracy Levine
    Flower Mound TX
69. Rose Nelson
    Greenville NC
70. Christy Anana
    Snohomish WA
71. Shaddy
    Beloit WI
72. Michelle Blackman
    De Pere WI
73. John Cahill
    N Bethesda MD
74. Andrew Phillips
    Cary NC
75. Kathleen Palm
    Woodburn IN
76. Court Johnson
    Montecito CA
77. Linda Barnes
    Wilmington NC
78. Bonnie Taylor
    Gig Harbor WA
79. Gillian Colley
    Hanover PA
80. Lucille Wood-Trost
    Bellingham WA
81. M. G. Chai
    East Amherst NY
82. David K. Bishop
    Colorado Springs CO
83. Philip Clark
    Calgary AB Canada
84. Janice Alonso
    Alpharetta GA
85. Janelle Bitikofer
    Raleigh NC
86. Sarah Porter
    Claremont NH
87. Brent Bachiu
    Regina SK Canada
88. Elizabeth Dulemba
    Avondale Estates GA
89. Oz Parvaiz
    Richmond VA
90. Amber McRee Turner
    Germantown TN
91. Jamie Purdy
    Victor MT
92. Will Wright
    Winston-Salem NC
93. Dana Konop
    Canton GA
94. Jean Reagan
    Salt Lake City UT
95. Avery Anderson
    Ridgecrest CA
96. Angela De Groot
    Cherry Hill NJ
97. Amy Chiasson
    Waltham MA
98. Nancy LaTurner
    Albuquerque NM
99. Sarah Watson
    Ridgefield CT
100. Avery Anderson
     Ridgecrest CA

FEATURE ARTICLE WINNERS

1. Katie McCollow
   Minneapolis MN
2. Carla Occaso
   Lyndonville VT
3. Dena Blatt
   Anacortes WA
4. Bo Yu
   Portland OR
5. Victor Englebert
   Allentown PA
6. Chelsea Kellner
   Freeport PA
7. Roberta Roberti
   Brooklyn NY
8. Richard Methia
   Fairfax Station VA
9. Leonide Martin
   Sammamish WA
10. Xujun Eberlein
    Wayland MA
11. Melissa Fry
    Mammoth AZ
12. John Worlton
    New York NY
13. Jill Richardson
    Warrenville IL
14. Jeremy Walton
    Warminster, Wiltshire United Kingdom
15. Melissa Hantman
    Pittsford NY
16. Kathy Casteel
    Auxvasse MO
17. Larry McMullen
    Bensalem PA
18. Arlene Weslowsky
    Morinville AB Canada
19. Suzette Pruitt
    Houston TX
20. Jenny Ruth Yasi
    Peaks Island ME
21. Thomas S. Doppke
    Sterling Heights MI
22. Carolyn Creedon
    Saint Louis MO
23. Cynthia Long
    Arlington VA
24. Barry Friedman
    Tulsa OK
25. Sam Morton
    Columbia SC
26. Victor Kamenir
    Sherwood OR
27. Barry Friedman
    Tulsa OK
28. Adrienne Dyer
    Brentwood Bay BC Canada
29. Ted Conigliaro
    Naples FL
30. Maureen Arges Nadin
    Thunder Bay ON Canada
31. Sherry Saturno
    Tarrytown NY
32. John Moir
    Santa Cruz CA
33. John W. Beck
    Santa Cruz CA
34. Julie W Henig
    Santa Rosa CA
35. John Henry Sotomayor
    Ocala FL
36. Alexander C. Congrove
    Roseville CA
37. Jennifer Van Evra
    Vancouver BC Canada
38. Anne Kelly
    Charlevoix MI
39. John Henry Sotomayor
    Stephen Robitaille
    Heather Lee
    Ocala FL
40. Zaina Arafat
    McLean VA
41. Robert Bowers
    Hurricane WV
42. Patricia Luce Chapman
    Rockport TX
43. Jennifer Lacey
    Minneola FL
44. Chanin Preece
    Cheyenne WY
45. Laurel Pesez
    Kerrville TX
46. Alex Gabbard
    Lenoir City TN
47. Steve Tarter
    Peoria IL
48. Steven Nesbit
    Lancaster PA
49. Kim O'Connell
    Arlington VA
50. Kathleen Wilson Shryock
    Olathe KS
51. Patricia Corcoran
    New Milford CT
52. Jennifer Mackey Stewart
    Round Rock TX
53. Kim Koenig
    Damascus OR
54. Russell W. Estlack
    St. George UT
55. Danelle Carvell
    Halifax PA
56. Marge Hartung
    Fairmont WV
57. Jack Lintelmann
    Buhl ID
58. Robert A. Lindblom
    United Kingdom
59. Anne Pawli
    Montague MI
60. Lisa K. Parsons
    Portland OR
61. Jenna Rose Robbins
    Playa del Rey CA
62. Barbara Anton
    Sarasota FL
63. John Culpepper
    Fort Worth TX
64. Jennifer B. Thompson
    Marion IA
65. Brian Trent
    Waterbury CT
66. Susan Palmquist
    Eden Prairie MN
67. Kim Brown
    Yreka CA
68. Jennifer Van Evra
    Vancouver BC Canada
69. George D. Wood
    Wilbraham MA
70. JaLeen Bultman-Deardurff
    Rensselaer IN
71. Lynn Wallen
    Manitowoc WI
72. Lucy Jokiel
    Honolulu HI
73. Geri Hoekzema
    Vancouver WA
74. Janet Mendelsohn
    West Somerville MA
75. Robert Seelenfreund
    West Orange NJ
76. Jo McDowell
    Brunswick GA
77. Brunetta Two Lenz
    Las Vegas NV
78. Miriam Filler
    Skokie IL
79. Deanna Hershiser
    Eugene OR
80. Lois Elfman
    New York NY
81. Greg Waxberg
    Ridgeland MS
82. Nancy J. Kauffman
    Fleetwood PA
83. Felicia Lowenstein Niven
    Northfield NJ
84. Jennifer Lacey
    Minneola FL
85. Jack Lintelmann
    Buhl ID
86. Adrienne Dyer
    Brentwood Bay BC Canada
87. Irene A. Harkleroad
    Carefree AZ
88. Eddy Rogers
    Houston TX
89. Mary Ann Masesar
    Vancouver BC Canada
90. Ramsey Harris
    Athens GA
91. Christy Heitger
    Bloomington IN
92. John Buchner
    Whiting NJ
93. Anna M. Elias
    Orlando FL
94. Janet Park
    Seattle WA
95. Holly Bellebuono
    Chilmark MA
96. Andrew Gregory Krzak
    New Lenox IL
97. Hugh Neeld
    Jacksonville TX
98. Jim Witty
    Bend OR
99. Martha R. Fehl
    Brookville IN
100. Michelle Lovato
     Pinon Hills CA

GENRE SHORT STORY WINNERS

1. Suzanne Burns
   Bend OR
2. Kristal M. Johnson
   LaGrangeville NY
3. Heather Ricks
   Snellville GA
4. Robert Rodden
   Peoria IL
5. David Larson
   Asheville NC
6. Ann Maltese
   Sicklerville NJ
7. Michael J. Mac Turk
   Orchard Park NY
8. Robert A. Lindblom
   United Kingdom
9. Matthew W. Vickers
   Penn Valley CA
10. Mark Moronell, MD FACC
    Anchorage AK
11. Mark Moronell, MD FACC
    Anchorage AK
12. Barbara J. Leonard
    Pageland SC
13. Kathy DeCotis
    Cranston RI
14. Pamela S. Beason
    Bellingham WA
15. Janet Brett
    Fairland OK
16. William R. Harris
    Frederick MD
17. Jeff Stinson
    El Dorado AR
18. Nikki Deckon
    Wilsonville OR
19. Mark E. Daugherty
    Staunton VA
20. Roger Norman Coe
    Hilton Head Island SC
21. Kelly L. Barnes-McCue
    Clovis CA
22. Camille Garrett
    Germantown MD
23. Lilia Ferreira
    North York ON Canada
24. Robert Chute
    London ON Canada
25. Robert Chute
    London ON Canada
26. Anna Elias
    Orlando FL
27. Sheri McGuinn
    Lakeside AZ
28. Craig Faris
    Rock Hill SC
29. Jennifer Sober
    Hampstead MD
30. Gabriella Herkert
    Everett WA
31. Lou Dean
    Ponca City OK
32. Carol A. Peterson
    River Falls WI
33. Belinda Frisch
    Ballston Spa NY
34. Christa Krais
    Allen TX
35. Janice Burns
    Mary Esther FL
36. D. Michael Ball
    Aurora IL
37. John Schultz
    Seattle WA
38. Teri Allen
    Grants Pass OR
39. Charles Hightower
    Montgomery AL
40. L. Guy LeVee
    Eldersburg MD
41. Lori Cecil
    Centerburg OH
42. Keith Casey
    Lockport NY
43. Michael Kanuckel
    Killbuck OH
44. Susan Redmond
    Newark OH
45. Ray Clark
    Goole United Kingdom
46. Stephanie Burkhart
    Castaic CA
47. Kathy Ferrell Powell
    Richardson TX
48. Claire L. Brouhard
    Lakewood CO
49. Joe Bean
    Leeds United Kingdom
50. Laura Khan
    Brooklyn NY
51. Kristal M. Johnson
    LaGrangeville NY
52. James Bergstad
    Hendersonville NC
53. Michael Simon
    Saint John NB Canada
54. Rita Nesbitt
    Trinity TX
55. John P. Buentello
    San Antonio TX
56. Jean Conklin
    Shoreview MN
57. Peg Snyder
    Sun Prairie WI
58. Vance Hatch
    Claremont CA
59. JT Gregory
    San Diego CA
60. Michael Woodall
    Portland OR
61. Kathy Johnson
    Richfield MN
62. Nathan Berg
    Aberdeen SD
63. Wayne and Treba Thompson
    Hoover AL
64. Susan Budavari
    Fountain Hills AZ
65. Martha (Marti) Costello
    McDonough GA
66. Sandra L. Vardaman
    Indianapolis IN
67. Flora Reekstin
    Littleton CO
68. Teresa Little
    Jacksonville FL
69. Julie Burroughs
    Hilton Head Island SC
70. Dennis Jankowski
    Perry Hall MD
71. Phyllis Smallman
    Salt Spring Is.BC Canada
72. Christine Guthmiller
    Kanawha IA
73. Matthew Peterson
    Peoria AZ
74. Lorie Brallier
    Los Osos CA
75. Rhonda Benthin
    Southern Pines NC
76. Hannah Metheny
    Boxborough MA
77. Donald L. Will
    Mount Vernon WA
78. Gregory Joseph
    South Elgin IL
79. Jim L. Pope
    Greeley CO
80. Lois Mintah
    Washington IL
81. Alan Naditz
    Sacramento CA
82. Catherine A. Adams
    Beach City OH
83. Paul McAllister
    Blue Island IL
84. Ellen Straw
    Covina CA
85. Michelle (Shelly) L. Grogan
    Eugene OR
86. David Scott
    Morehead KY
87. Donna Mason
    West Lorne ON Canada
88. Benjamin H. Foreman
    Port Orange FL
89. Francis D. Homer
    Wellsville NY
90. Ramya Sethuraman
    Lexington KY
91. Donna Marie Taylor
    Emerson NJ
92. Allan Stewart
    Melbourne, Victoria Australia
93. James Cousins
    Dorset United Kingdom
94. Christopher S. Montgomery
    Joliet IL
95. Jayne Lytle
    North Stratford NH
96. Martha Culp
    Johnson City TN
97. Rick Barry
    Plainfield IN
98. Janice Cutbush
    Ballston Spa NY
99. John Bujanowski, Jr.
    Fort Edward NY
100. Aaron Cobb
     Dunmor KY

INSPIRATIONAL WRITING WINNERS

1. Bradley J. Gustafson
   Scottsbluff NE
2. Eric Witchey
   Salem OR
3. Kionna LeMalle
   Alexandria LA
4. Hannah Ketcham
   Dorr MI
5. Twyla Martin
   Grand Junction CO
6. Reynold Conger
   Belen NM
7. Lisa Peters
   Georgetown MA
8. Martha Lee Fuchs
   Dora AL
9. Kathleen Tresemer
   Rockton IL
10. Elainea Haynes
    Cleburne TX
11. Amanda Waters
    Wilmington NC
12. Gregg Koskela
    Newberg OR
13. Gina Mazza Hillier
    Harmony PA
14. Donald R. Ackermann
    Barnegat NJ
15. Cameron Coursey
    Defiance MO
16. Jeff Danelek
    Lakewood CO
17. Irena Tervo
    Simpsonville SC
18. Jordan Browning
    Princeton Junction NJ
19. Susan Matthews
    Huntingdon Valley PA
20. Merri Manetzke
    Eureka MO
21. Beverly Varnado
    Athens GA
22. Maryann Martinsen
    Layton UT
23. Fred Stewart
    Eagleville PA
24. Kim A. Talbert
    Keller TX
25. Renee Quirion
    Windsor ME
26. Jennifer Hinders
    Fairfax VA
27. Richard Wile
    Yarmouth ME
28. Caroleah Johnson
    Berry Creek CA
29. K. C. Mosier II
    Santa Fe NM
30. Julie Everett
    Shorewood WI
31. Julie Everett
    Shorewood WI
32. David Maidment
    Nantwich Cheshire United Kingdom
33. Ruth Gulbranson
    Blaine MN
34. Dolores A. McCabe
    Hamden NY
35. Rebecca Lee Williams
    Madison WI
36. Mal King
    Santa Paula CA
37. Thomas X. Parman
    Bronson FL
38. Thomas X. Parman
    Bronson FL
39. Lou Dean
    Ponca City OK
40. Lauren Carson
    East Falmouth MA
41. Marguerite Gray
    Ferriday LA
42. Michael Anderson
    Lake Elmo MN
43. Myra Fozard
    Aliquippa PA
44. Edith Schloss Jacobs
    Sarasota FL
45. Hazel P. Pope
    Grand Bay AL
46. Danelle Carvell
    Halifax PA
47. Mal King
    Santa Paula CA
48. Gary Griffin
    Campbell TX
49. Kristen L. Tompkins
    Rochester NY
50. Jenna Fontaine
    Asheville NC
51. Colleen Benedict
    Thousand Oaks CA
52. Hazel P. Pope
    Grand Bay AL
53. Shirley Gerdes
    New Braunfels TX
54. Martha Lee Fuchs
    Dora AL
55. L. S. Cherokee
    Rainier WA
56. David Chick
    Westford MA
57. Robin Rogel
    Nappanee IN
58. Charlotte Hofer
    Sioux Falls SD
59. Marcy Kennedy
    Wallaceburg ON Canada
60. Ruth Truman
    Camarillo CA
61. Linda Jo Reed
    Spokane WA
62. Cherilyn DeAguero
    San Clemente CA
63. Susan Jennings
    Bluemont VA
64. Gina Wahlen
    Silang, Cavite Philippines
65. Beverly Varnado
    Athens GA
66. Jennifer Allen
    Mebane NC
67. Michael Kochanski
    Bensenville IL
68. Roberta Kelm
    Sunnyvale CA
69. Rhonda Larson
    Soldotna AK
70. Patricia Price
    Grayslake IL
71. Sue Culver
    Bellevue WA
72. Barbara K. Henderson
    Oakland NJ
73. Yvette M. Leach
    Cibolo TX
74. Ken McGee
    Louisburg NC
75. Patricia Casey
    Spencerport NY
76. Betty Jo Bochy
    Billings MT
77. Kathy Ferrell Powell
    Richardson TX
78. Niki Nymark
    St. Louis MO
79. Leslie Joan Linder
    Penobscot ME
80. Leah Weiss
    Lynchburg VA
81. Carly Kimmel
    Los Angeles CA
82. Bonnie Grove
    Saskatoon SK Canada
83. Emily Conrad
    Oshkosh WI
84. Laura Pannell
    Richmond VA
85. Andrea Prescott
    Willamina OR
86. Linda Tyrol
    Helsinki Finland
87. David D. Miller
    Saint Charles MO
88. Alexandra Parsons
    New York NY
89. Frank Ball
    Fort Worth TX
90. Rebecca A. Givens
    Calera AL
91. Gem Bomhower
    Virginia Beach VA
92. Vicki Phipps
    Lampasas TX
93. Susan Rakowski
    Germantown TN
94. Laura S. Faeth
    Superior CO
95. Mary D. Transue
    Dahlonega GA
96. Alina Patterson
    Altamonte Springs FL
97. Patricia Boysen
    Orange Park FL
98. Kenneth L. Nolen
    King City CA
99. Betty N. Wright
    Lakeville NB Canada
100. Matthew Peterson
     Peoria AZ

MAINSTREAM/LITERARY SHORT STORY WINNERS

1. Jeff McCormick
   Lakeland FL
2. Kathryn MacDonald
   Bainbridge Island WA
3. James Gish, Jr.
   Arcanum OH
4. Alexa I. Stefanou
   State College PA
5. Scarlett Annadeus Baker
   Austin TX
6. Robert George
   Denver CO
7. Evan Pickering
   Amityville NY
8. Kenneth W. Plumb
   Lenexa KS
9. R. E. Wood
   Patchogue NY
10. Michael Mort
    Arlington VA
11. Alice Louise Wagoner
    Roswell NM
12. R. E. Wood
    Patchogue NY
13. Peg Elliott Mayo
    Blodgett OR
14. Marcia Corbino
    Sarasota FL
15. Candy Davis
    Cottage Grove OR
16. Madison Taylor-Hayden
    Wausau WI
17. Fred Joshu
    Saint Charles MO
18. Richard Gibney
    Sutton Co Dublin Ireland
19. Beryl MacDonald
    Salem OR
20. Sarah Frances Hardy
    Oxford MS
21. Sabine French
    Raleigh NC
22. Jo Lauer
    Santa Rosa CA
23. Erika Napoletano
    Las Vegas NV
24. Hasmik Arakelyan
    San Francisco CA
25. Thomas M. Hill
    Tucson AZ
26. Angelo Talluto
    Manchester NJ
27. Robin S. Crawford
    Mentor-on-the-Lake OH
28. Jessica Paul
    Richmond VA
29. Alicia Stankay
    Ambridge PA
30. Melanie Griffin
    North Augusta SC
31. Jay DeVane
    Greensboro NC
32. Chrissy K. McVay
    Little Switzerland NC
33. Chrissy K. McVay
    Little Switzerland NC
34. Aaron B. Donner
    Bay Shore NY
35. Anne Welsh
    Kilauea HI
36. Nikki Andrews
    Wilton NH
37. Dean Stewart
    Sylmar CA
38. Ralph G. (Jerry) Stevenson
    Pueblo CO
39. Zola Stultz
    Portal AZ
40. Catherine P. Snider
    Portland OR
41. Carol Wobig
    Milwaukee WI
42. Elena Iglesias
    Miami FL
43. Patsy Evans Pittman
    Vienna WV
44. E. R. Dillon
    Ponchatoula LA
45. Joanne M. Moore
    Raleigh NC
46. Blaise Buchowski
    Seattle WA
47. Lauren Carson
    East Falmouth MA
48. Mark Cowlin
    Denver CO
49. Jennifer Byrne
    Glassboro NJ
50. Patsy Evans Pittman
    Vienna WV
51. Lillian E. Hans
    Aurora CO
52. Donna L. Paullin
    Oakland CA
53. Tori Bond
    Perkasie PA
54. Sharon L. Howard
    Charlottesville VA
55. Marcel Bally
    Shirley NY
56. Irena Travo
    Simpsonville SC
57. Donna Mitchell
    Lake Oswego OR
58. Glen A. Ross
    Bellevue NE
59. Sioban Gallagher
    Midlothian VA
60. John Irwin
    Rohnert Park CA
61. Charles Schaeffer
    Bethesda MD
62. Cecelia (Cecile) Calmes
    Woodland CA
63. Kathryn MacDonald
    Bainbridge Island WA
64. Sioban Gallagher
    Midlothian VA
65. George Partridge
    Osoyoos BC Canada
66. Lauren B. Grossman
    Tucson AZ
67. Daniela Gibson
    San Francisco CA
68. Kerry Petrichek
    Finleyville PA
69. Christine Kephart
    Toms River NJ
70. Bonnie Burnatowski
    Pennellville NY
71. Bob Knapp
    Baltimore MD
72. Charlie Elliott
    Lafayette LA
73. Trent England
    Brighton MA
74. Elsie Schmied Knoke
    Oak Ridge TN
75. Cecily Hamlin Wells
    Hendersonville NC
76. James H. Henry
    Longview TX
77. Patrick Sean Lee
    Mission Viejo CA
78. Lisa F. Vargas
    Dunn NC
79. Gloria Hutchinson
    Glenburn ME
80. Liz Sawyer
    Marysville CA
81. Thomas Fullmer
    Salt Lake City UT
82. Suzanne M. Garrity
    Princeton MA
83. Richard Kigel
    Staten Island NY
84. Dorian Tilbury
    Brooklyn NY
85. Angela Kriger
    Fife WA
86. Barbara D. Hall
    Wayne NJ
87. Mindy Sitton-Halleck
    Bothell WA
88. Margaret E. Holeman
    Hope AK
89. Alysia Lyons
    Falls Church VA
90. Jennifer Hermann
    Arcadia CA
91. Jeffrey C. Bowser
    Grove City PA
92. Jodi Buchan
    Bemidji MN
93. Connie F. Crowe-Miller
    Kihei HI
94. Andrew Zembles
    Corona Del Mar CA
95. Virginia Kupferman
    Albuquerque NM
96. Cheryl Renée Grossman
    Toronto ON Canada
97. Lori McFerran
    Alburtis PA
98. Evelyn Goodrick
    Charleston IL
99. Barbara D. Hall
    Wayne NJ
100. Ted Shrader
     San Antonio TX

MEMOIR/PERSONAL ESSAY WINNERS

1. Todd Gauchat with Deborah Burke
   Lakewood OH
2. Amanda Kelley
   Houston TX
3. Jayne Warren
   Farmerville LA
4. Noreen Lehmann
   Las Cruces NM
5. Sandra L. Staton-Taiwo
   York PA
6. Caren Gallimore
   Christiansburg VA
7. Caren Gallimore
   Christiansburg VA
8. Terry Miles
   Hoboken NJ
9. Elizabeth Dark Wiley
   West Tisbury MA
10. Scott Mason
    Raleigh NC
11. Pat Willy
    Portal AZ
12. Denise Heinze
    Durham NC
13. L. Marie Bernier
    Allen Park MI
14. L. Marie Bernier
    Allen Park MI
15. Scott Levinson
    Putnam Valley NY
16. Richard N. Valentine
    Palm Harbor FL
17. Jodi Bowersox
    Tonganoxie KS
18. Morna Murphy Martell
    Staten Island NY
19. Ron Stempkowski
    Chicago IL
20. Andrea Wilson
    Burbank CA
21. L. Marie Bernier
    Allen Park MI
22. Tex Shrader
    San Antonio TX
23. Miriam Fuller
    Skokie IL
24. Regina Smeltzer
    Darlington SC
25. Christopher Aragao
    Riverside RI
26. Ann Guaglione
    Commack NY
27. Holly Bellebuono
    Chilmark MA
28. Lisa Betz
    Gering NE
29. Crystal Rice
    Hagerstown MD
30. Carol Taylor
    Golden CO
31. Basil Balian
    Cincinnati OH
32. Patricia Twohig
    Corona CA
33. Paulle Clark
    El Prado NM
34. Robert Y. Ellis
    Rockport MA
35. Jessica Kennedy
    McKinney TX
36. James Steed
    Little Rock AR
37. Riley N. Kelly
    Excel AL
38. Sharri Chappell
    Nashville TN
39. Gloria G. Murray
    Deer Park NY
40. Dick Vojvoda
    Danville CA
41. Rozann Grunig
    Martinez CA
42. Morgan Barnhart
    Eugene OR
43. Cindy Gierhart
    Boston MA
44. Toni Faubion-Truesdell
    Palmer AK
45. Roberta Parker Martin
    Black Mountain NC
46. Libby Bishop
    San Antonio TX
47. Dorothy L. Ward
    Springfield ME
48. Linda S. Clare
    Eugene OR
49. Tara M. Bloom
    Portland OR
50. Carol Maupin
    Bowling Green KY
51. Marty Toohey
    Bloomfield Hills MI
52. Warren Briggs
    Pensacola FL
53. Daniel Burch Fiddler
    Idyllwild CA
54. Margi Lane
    Vancouver WA
55. Elizabeth Joanne Johns Johnson
    Jupiter FL
56. Jacqueline Clay Chester
    Atlanta GA
57. Scott Thompson
    Lawrenceville GA
58. Oliver French
    Brooktondale NY
59. Carol Brian
    Bend OR
60. Jenna Leitnaker
    Beavercreek OH
61. William A. Abbott
    Tacoma WA
62. Trudi A. Buck
    Ashaway RI
63. Kim Marie Jakway
    Syracuse NY
64. Adrienne Benson Scherger
    Syracuse NY
65. Jean Strong
    Springdale AR
66. Leah Weiss
    Lynchburg VA
67. Mary F. Dado
    Palm Harbor FL
68. Sheila Romano
    Elk Grove CA
69. Bill Jackson
    Paso Robles CA
70. Lou Dean
    Ponca City OK
71. Marty Toohey
    Bloomfield Hills MI
72. Jessica Kennedy
    McKinney TX
73. John West
    Cody WY
74. Bill Hartman
    Columbia Falls MT
75. Catherine Saliba
    East Brunswick NJ
76. Susan Jensen
    Clinton WA
77. Dave Copeland
    Burlington MA
78. Linda Dees
    Madison AL
79. J. M. Cornwell
    Colorado Springs CO
80. Homer L. Jackson
    Henryetta OK
81. Traci Mitchell
    Snohomish WA
82. Marleen Guess
    Solana Beach CA
83. Melanie Carroll
    Kailua HI
84. James Steed
    Little Rock AR
85. Diana Ferguson
    Grove City OH
86. Jane F. Rudden
    Lancaster PA
87. Nyki Anello
    Tucson AZ
88. Dana Laquidara
    Upton MA
89. Sama Bears Rubin
    Avenel NJ
90. Valerie Katagiri
    Beaverton OR
91. Samantha Thacker
    Bayside NY
92. Dawn Haines
    Dover NH
93. Karen Berliner
    Airmont NY
94. Loren Martz
    Long Beach NY
95. Suzanna Quintana
    Sheridan WY
96. Art Rogers
    Dallas TX
97. Audrey Roberts
    Madison WI
98. Joan Miller
    San Leandro CA
99. Lorene A. Hermann
    Three Rivers MI
100. Caitlin Friree
    Los Angeles CA

NON-RHYMING POETRY WINNERS

1. Alison Luterman — Oakland CA
2. Maria Ercilla — Los Angeles CA
3. Sheila A. Murphy — Portland CT
4. Christine Houser — Crystal Beach FL
5. Maria Ercilla — Los Angeles CA
6. Ann Tsao — Charlotte NC
7. Diana Dominguez — Brownsville TX
8. Dennis Rhodes — Provincetown MA
9. Carol R. Gavounas — Dallas TX
10. Laura Imbimbo (pen name: Marie) — Sussex NJ
11. Sarah Elizabeth Mills — Dover DE
12. Cheryl A. Martin — Canton MI
13. Enid Graf — Stony Brook NY
14. Doug Thiele — Norfolk VA
15. Annabelle Moseley — Dix Hills NY
16. Annabelle Moseley — Dix Hills NY
17. Annabelle Moseley — Dix Hills NY
18. Melissa Favara — Brooklyn NY
19. Sheila A. Murphy — Portland CT
20. Freda Westman — Juneau AK
21. Gloria Masterson-Richardson — Rockport MA
22. Bonnie Idowu — Manassas VA
23. Dianalee Velie — Newbury NH
24. Yvette Morales — Long Island City NY
25. Deborah McGroder — Cleveland OH
26. Marianne Betterly — Kensington CA
27. Maria Ercilla — Los Angeles CA
28. Maria Ercilla — Los Angeles CA
29. Susan Jensen — Clinton WA
30. Holly Chiron — Seattle WA
31. Marla Alupoaicei — Frisco TX
32. Edward W. Lull — Williamsburg VA
33. Barbara Ryder Levinson — Azusa CA
34. Claire J. Baker — Pinole CA
35. Debra Simpson — Eldersburg MD
36. Christine J. Lloyd — Colorado Springs CO
37. Stacy Campbell — Hurst TX
38. Laura Graham Miller — Los Angeles CA
39. Shirley Smith Wilbert — Columbia MO
40. Rudy Mancini — Calistoga CA
41. Maria Ercilla — Los Angeles CA
42. Sarah Lauderdale — Huntley IL
43. Kathryn Hutchison — Palatine IL
44. Amber Nolan — Brooklyn NY
45. Tracie — Detroit MI
46. Maria Ercilla — Los Angeles CA
47. Monique Lewis — Endwell NY
48. Rachel Nixon — Topeka KS
49. Tracey Cowenhoven — Bakersfield CA
50. Patricia LaBarbera — Homestead FL
51. Patricia LaBarbera — Homestead FL
52. Dallas Huth — Santa Fe NM
53. Patricia LaBarbera — Homestead FL
54. Michael Leggs — St. Paul MN
55. Thomas McCroskey — Walland TN
56. Sanje James — Bronx NY
57. Sarah Nelson — Perth ON Canada
58. Gawaine Caldwater Ross — Marlboro MA
59. Marianne Y. Ray — Kent WA
60. Dallas Huth — Santa Fe NM
61. Gary Hill — Bakersfield CA
62. Albert H. deAprix — Scotia NY
63. Andrew B. Pierce — Miami FL
64. Glen Dalrymple — Lancaster PA
65. Judith Stephens — Richmond CA
66. Dianalee Velie — Newbury NH
67. Thomas Ray Fullmer — Salt Lake City UT
68. Maria Ercilla — Los Angeles CA
69. Bonnie Idowu — Manassas VA
70. Bonnie Idowu — Manassas VA
71. Jonathan Simons — Boulder CO
72. Anne Say Lau — Granada Hills CA
73. Stefanie Yoko Sakamoto — Honolulu HI
74. Annabelle Moseley — Dix Hills NY
75. Lee Tupman — Orleans MA
76. Lee Tupman — Orleans MA
77. Annabelle Moseley — Dix Hills NY
78. Annabelle Moseley — Dix Hills NY
79. Sheryl L. Nelms — Clyde TX
80. Verna Lee Hinegardner — Hot Springs AR
81. Bonnie Idowu — Manassas VA
82. JoAnne Gottlieb — Henderson NV
83. Margaret Morris — Leesburg FL
84. Kim S. Neese — Farmerville LA
85. Jamila Hammad — Christiansted Virgin Islands
86. Melissa Favara — Brooklyn NY
87. David Prinz Hufford — Omaha NE
88. Gary Hill — Bakersfield CA
89. Brian Trent — Prospect CT
90. J. Graham Ducker — Oshawa ON Canada
91. Marilyn Arvizo — Long Beach CA
92. Ann Tsao — Charlotte NC
93. Ann Tsao — Charlotte NC
94. Mary Ranieri — Gonzales TX
95. Ruth Weiner — Deerfield Beach FL
96. Kathleen Whitman Plucker — Bloomington IN
97. Anne Martinez — Great Falls MT
98. Phyllis Cobb — Villanova PA
99. Jean B. Fleischauer — Pittsburgh PA
100. Anne-Marie Legan — Herrin IL

RHYMING POETRY WINNERS

1. James Anderson
North Miami FL
2. Amanda Nazario
New York NY
3. Luise Putcamp Jr.
Albuquerque NM
4. Michelle Garvin
Ocean Park WA
5. Herb Wahlsteen
Farmingville NY
6. Robert Daseler
Davis CA
7. Wayne Lee
Santa Fe NM
8. Karin Bradberry
Albuquerque NM
9. Anna Amatuzio
New York NY
10. Susan Childress
Holland MI
11. Marla Alupoaicei
Frisco TX
12. Anita Kasabova
Sofia Bulgaria
13. Carolyn Creedon
Saint Louis MO
14. Robert Daseler
Davis CA
15. Elisabeth Schechter
Bryn Mawr PA
16. N. Colwell Snell
Salt Lake City UT
17. Patricia Callan
Newton MA
18. Charles Brashear
Corvallis OR
19. Marilyn Bentov
Newton MA
20. Robert Daseler
Davis CA
21. Robert Daseler
Davis CA
22. Lindrith Davies
Brooks ME
23. Valma M. Bartlett
Oak Harbor WA
24. Fabio Cardoso
Honolulu HI
25. Sharon L. Howard
Charlottesville VA
26. Herb Wahlsteen
Farmingville NY
27. Joan Higuchi
West Islip NY
28. Herb Wahlsteen
Farmingville NY
29. Herb Wahlsteen
Farmingville NY
30. Nelson Blish
Rochester NY
31. E. Shaun Russell
Burnaby BC Canada
32. Lynn Veach Sadler
Sanford NC
33. Robert Daseler
Davis CA
34. N. Colwell Snell
Salt Lake City UT
35. Patricia Luce Chapman
Rockport TX
36. Robert Daseler
Davis CA
37. Anita Kasabova
Sofia Bulgaria
38. Jimi
Englewood CO
39. Ronda Lawson
Castro Valley CA
40. Michele Oster
Rocky Point NY
41. Vonnie Coleman
Palm Harbor FL
42. Dianne Borsenik
Elyria OH
43. Kula
44. Ryan Tilley
Longwood FL
45. Cordell Caudron
Lewiston ID
46. Dena R. Gorrell
Edmond OK
47. Jimi
Englewood CO
48. Tonya Taliaferro
Baltimore MD
49. Gary McGregor
Hattiesburg MS
50. Karen Murray Broadhead
Ellsworth WI
51. Shala Kean
Dansville MI
52. M. D. Puzzuoli
Westland MI
53. Sandra Kasturi
Toronto ON Canada
54. N. Colwell Snell
Salt Lake City UT
55. N. Colwell Snell
Salt Lake City UT
56. Michael Anthony McDonough
Ballston Spa NY
57. N. Colwell Snell
Salt Lake City UT
58. Pam Rhodes
Corinth MS
59. Jessica Weed
Fulton MO
60. Patricia Callan
Newton MA
61. Patricia Callan
Newton MA
62. Robert Daseler
Davis CA
63. Graham Kash
Cookeville TN
64. Karin Bradberry
Albuquerque NM
65. Jacquelyn Lansing
Escondido CA
66. Diane Borsenik
Elyria OH
67. Erin Bayne
Tampa FL
68. N. Colwell Snell
Salt Lake City UT
69. Candice
Houston TX
70. Debbie Pea
Eden Prairie MN
71. Kristin Mast
Loveland CO
72. Sherri Boyd
Thief River Falls MN
73. Mary Miller
Broken Arrow OK
74. Kevin Pace
Greenfield IN
75. Barbara Blanks
Garland TX
76. Jeketa Woods
Gastonia NC
77. Allie McComas
Centerville OH
78. Lisa Lawston
Amherst MA
79. Dhruv K. Singhal
Dallas TX
80. Nelson Blish
Rochester NY
81. Michael Mackey
Norfolk VA
82. Julia Rose Statzer
Mishawaka IN
83. Martha J. Lee
Hudson NH
84. Joe Sharp
Orange VA
85. Andrew B. Pierce
Miami FL
86. John Irwin
Rohnert Park CA
87. Dianne Borsenik
Elyria OH
88. Mary Owens
Crab Orchard KY
89. Anne Johnson Mullin
New Harbor ME
90. Matthew Simmons
Florence SC
91. Debra Smith
Rienzi MS
92. Jim Allen
Elkhart IN
93. Doris Lockhart
Dallas TX
94. Donna L. Barnes
Columbia MO
95. Rachel Fullilove
San Diego CA
96. Jeffrey Kuczmarski
Chicago IL
97. Kathleen Walker
Mount Airy MD
98. Jacquelyn Lansing
Escondido CA
99. Jacquelyn Lansing
Escondido CA
100. Jim Allen
Elkhart IN

STAGE PLAY WINNERS

1. Don Orwald
   Granbury TX
2. Catherine Rust
   Toronto ON Canada
3. Maria Rokas
   San Francisco CA
4. Jim Gustafson
   Wheaton IL
5. Tom Mercer
   Martinez CA
6. Justin Cioppa
   Wilmington NC
7. Joseph Horst
   Winterville NC
8. Cyndie Goins Hoelscher
   Corpus Christi TX
9. Kari Catton Anderson
   Springfield IL
10. William Pugsley
    North Hollywood CA
11. Tencha Avila
    Denver CO
12. Justin Cioppa
    Wilmington NC
13. Brent Englar
    Hermosa Beach CA
14. Jaynie Roberts
    Vancouver WA
15. Lainie Marsh
    Whites Creek TN
16. Kathleen Ann Nett
    Hillsboro WI
17. Doris M. Matern
    Fairview TX
18. Leslie Stevenson
    Scotland UK
19. Don Quiett
    Fuquay-Varina NC
20. Martha Humphreys
    Huntsville AL
21. Michael Harrington
    Cambridge MA
22. Stacey Luftig
    New York NY
23. Jennifer Bogush
    Cranford NJ
24. Leona Nicholas Welch
    Fosters AL
25. M. Scott Johnson
    Tucson AZ
26. Katie L. Carroll
    Milford CT
27. Jacob M. Appel
    New York NY
28. Jen Wilding
    Chicago IL
29. Mark Lambeck
    Stratford CT
30. Robert Gately
    Bethlehem PA
31. Cynthia Lewis Ferrell
    Oak Park CA
32. Monica Michell
    Wimberley TX
33. Phillip Schmiedl
    New York NY
34. Kathleen Conner Combass
    Keystone Heights FL
35. Patricia Wakely Wolf
    Sherman Oaks CA
36. Paullette MacDougal
    Edwards CO
37. Barbara Lewis
    Chicago IL
38. Doris M. Matern
    Fairview TX
39. Linda Mitchell
    New Albany MS
40. Michael S. Parsons
    Columbus OH
41. Steven Somkin
    New York NY
42. Robert Gately
    Bethlehem PA
43. Edward Hartman
    Pipestem WV
44. Brian Bartels
    New York NY
45. Sy Huff
    San Francisco CA
46. Bill Wellborn
    Lawrenceville GA
47. Anne Phelan
    New York NY
48. Dawn T. Hilton
    Charlotte NC
49. Laura Richardson
    Van Nuys CA
50. Joel Herskowitz
    Natick MA
51. Bonnie K. Stevens
    Findlay OH
52. Robert Daseler
    Davis CA
53. Blair Whitney
    Springfield IL
54. Lazarre Seymour Simckes
    New Haven CT
55. James Del Fiore
    Alexandria VA
56. Dawn T. Hilton
    Charlotte NC
57. Tiffany Antone
    Los Angeles CA
58. Andrew Hinderaker
    Chicago IL
59. Jordan Owen
    Tucker GA
60. Hope Yeager
    Custer SD
61. Dennis E. Rager
    Bronx NY
62. Joe G. Hardin
    Mobile AL
63. Kathleen Conner Combass
    Keystone Heights FL
64. Brandon Kalbaugh
    Brooklyn NY
65. Peter Budka
    New York NY
66. James Edward Henderson
    Renton WA
67. Jody Houser
    Hollywood CA
68. Neville Mur
    Saint Louis MO
69. Shannan E. Johnson
    Tallahassee FL
70. Ken Curtis
    New York NY
71. Doris Lockhart
    Dallas TX
72. Anne Kern
    Eugene OR
73. Jaclyn Villano
    Portland ME
74. James A. Marzo
    Chappaqua NY
75. Richard Manley
    New York NY
76. B. D. Tharp
    Wichita KS
77. Donald Petty
    New York NY
78. Judith Stephens
    Richmond CA
79. Dee Hogan
    Devin Weissenbach
    Leavenworth KS
80. Eileen Dawson Peterson
    Eugene OR
81. Elaine Smith
    Sunnyside NY
82. Barbara Lewis
    Chicago IL
83. Jaelle Draigomir
    Ashland OR
84. Michael C. Reimann
    Orlando FL
85. Linda Wiges
    Traer IA
86. Darren Canady
    Brooklyn NY
87. Kim Brundidge
    East Point GA
88. Brandon Kalbaugh
    Brooklyn NY
89. William Breen
    Sacramento CA
90. Kathleen A. McLaughlin
    La Mesa CA
91. E. R. Dillon
    Ponchatoula LA
92. Lew Osteen
    Sacramento CA
93. Don Orwald
    Granbury TX
94. Richard Lenz
    Van Nuys CA
95. Fred de Luna
    West Linn OR
96. Carlos J. Serrano
    Bronx NY
97. A. H. Oberholtzer
    Santa Monica CA
98. T. B. Fisher
    Peninsula OH
99. Jan Henson Dow
    Bluffton SC
100. Ronald Draftina
    Jeannette PA

TELEVISION/MOVIE SCRIPT WINNERS

1. **Maureen Olund**
Houston, TX
2. **Stephan Cox**
Brentwood CA
3. **Joseph Harness**
Tuckerton NJ
4. **Julie Anne Wight**
Los Angeles CA
5. **Tyler Voss**
Fallon NV
6. **Louaine Collier Elke**
Walnut Creek CA
7. **Tom Lavagnino**
Los Angeles CA
8. **Christopher Acosta**
Hattiesburg MS
9. **Keisha Poiro**
Great Mills MD
10. **Leigh Fenty**
Michael Leath
Etna CA
11. **Kim Mankey**
Camp Hill PA
12. **Neil Citrin**
Santa Monica CA
13. **Keisha Poiro**
Great Mills MD
14. **Larry K. Meredith**
Gunnison CO
15. **C. J. Fletcher**
Denver CO
16. **Fred McGavran**
Cincinnati OH
17. **Lee Welch**
Kershaw SC
18. **Laura Covello**
Ulster Park NY
19. **Connie Corcoran Wilson**
Chicago IL
20. **Aaron J. Curtis**
Miami FL
21. **Daniel Ellis**
Ringgold GA
22. **Keisha Poiro**
Great Mills MD
23. **Robert Hill**
Franklin Square NY
24. **Carla Kanthak**
Chicago IL
25. **Granville Wyche Burgess**
Greenwich CT
26. **Keisha Poiro**
Great Mills MD
27. **C. J. Fletcher**
Denver CO
28. **Brian E. Grose**
Warrensville Hts OH
29. **William Frank Georgi**
Kalaheo HI
30. **Kathleen Pickering**
Fort Lauderdale FL
31. **Saba Igbe**
Kingston Jamaica
32. **Larry Edward Davis**
Garner NC
33. **James C. Burau**
Zach Hammill
St. Paul MN
34. **Felicia Ansty**
Ithaca NY
35. **Thomas L. Seltzer**
San Antonio TX
36. **Clarence Rolle**
Nassau Bahamas
37. **Dean Stewart**
Sylmar CA
38. **P. M. O'Malley**
Wheaton IL
39. **Thomas A. Mercer**
Martinez CA
40. **Sharon Dwyer**
Sorrento FL
41. **Ronnie Espinoza**
Miami FL
42. **Dave Green**
Tampa FL
43. **Paul Jensen**
Renton WA
44. **Matthew N. Irby**
Lewisville TX
45. **Andrew Jamison**
Vancouver WA
46. **Richard H. Kennedy**
Youngtown AZ
47. **Mike Schwartz**
Riverside CA
48. **C. V. Herst**
Oakland CA
49. **Johanna Burke**
Edgewater NJ
50. **Judith A. D'Ambrosia**
Playa Vista CA
51. **Mark Saunders**
Laredo TX
52. **Doris M. Matern**
Fairview TX
53. **Marc Calderwood**
Albuquerque NM
54. **Cindy Carroll**
Mississauga ON Canada
55. **Stephanee A. Leech**
Fenton MI
56. **Michael Dabney**
Indianapolis IN
57. **Andrew Gregory Krzak**
New Lenox IL
58. **Laird Roberts**
Bountiful UT
59. **Carl A. Veno**
Allentown PA
60. **Norman Bradford**
Tucson AZ
61. **John Ruemmler**
Charlottesville VA
62. **Daniel Mullins**
Troy OH
63. **Andrew Zins**
West Milton OH
64. **Hollie Overton**
Los Angeles CA
65. **Steven M. Cross**
Arcadia MO
66. **Oscar Hansen**
Mesa AZ
67. **John Nichols**
Oswego IL
68. **Magi Hart**
Eugene OR
69. **Keith M. Tracy**
Punta Gorda FL
70. **Barbara Garrett**
Los Angeles CA
71. **Patricia Rivers**
Troy NY
72. **Leigh Fenty**
Grenada CA
73. **M. Reyes**
New York NY
74. **Cynthia Blackledge**
Spring TX
75. **Erick Regaldo**
Fresno CA
76. **Dean Stewart**
Sylmar CA
77. **Scott & Paula Merrow**
Albuquerque NM
78. **C. J. Fletcher**
Denver CO
79. **Daniel A. Chomistek**
Medicine Hat AB Canada
80. **Debbie Taylor**
Denham Springs LA
81. **Bridget Bell Webber**
Annapolis MD
82. **Nicolaus Aufdenkampe**
Sunrise FL
83. **Cindy Carroll**
Mississauga ON Canada
84. **Ronald B. Petty, Sr.**
Orland CA
85. **Pamela M. Chase**
Guilford CT
86. **Carlo DeCarlo**
Rutherford NJ
87. **Mary Schultz**
Rio Rico AZ
88. **Laura Osborne**
Dedham MA
89. **Brian Trent**
Marty Lang
Prospect CT
90. **Eric Dawe**
Lansing MI
91. **Jeffry Weiss**
Boulder CO
92. **Bix Hopewell**
Los Angeles CA
93. **Deontrai Matthews**
Fort Wayne IN
94. **Laurie B. Turner**
Camarillo CA
95. **Steve Duncan**
Los Angeles CA
96. **Andru J. Reeve**
Martinez CA
97. **John J. Smith**
Plano TX
98. **Patricia Rivers**
Troy NY
99. **Kristina Smith**
Summerdale AL
100. **Lynda Hanna**
Virginia Beach VA

DISCOVER HOW EASY PUBLISHING YOUR BOOK CAN BE

Available at Amazon.com for $5.95 or as a free e-book at www.OutskirtsPress.com